Harry Collingwood

The Secret of the Sands, or, The 'Water Lily' and Her Crew

A Nautical Novel

Harry Collingwood

The Secret of the Sands, or, The 'Water Lily' and Her Crew
A Nautical Novel

ISBN/EAN: 9783337031763

Printed in Europe, USA, Canada, Australia, Japan

Cover: Foto ©Andreas Hilbeck / pixelio.de

More available books at **www.hansebooks.com**

OR,

THE "WATER LILY" AND HER CREW.

A NAUTICAL NOVEL.

BY

HARRY COLLINGWOOD.

IN TWO VOLUMES.
VOL. I.

GRIFFITH AND FARRAN,
CORNER OF ST. PAUL'S CHURCHYARD, LONDON.
1879.

PREFACE.

THE attention of the public has been directed, on more than one occasion within the last few years, to voyages of a more or less lengthy character, undertaken in craft of very small tonnage; and a great deal has been said and written concerning the foolhardiness of such undertakings. This, however, is more apparent than real, though much must necessarily depend, in such voyages, on the adventurer's skill as a seaman and his nerve and self-possession in critical moments. Almost, if not quite, as much will also depend upon the design, construction, and equipment of the craft in which such an adventure is undertaken; but where all these conditions are favourable, the actual danger may be reduced in quite a surprising degree.

Such voyages, however, if of any considerable length, are sure to abound in adventure ; and, in selecting one as the groundwork of my story, it has been my aim to endeavour at once to make it interesting and readable to those who have a liking for the sea and for nautical adventure, and to convey a few useful hints (gathered from my own experience) respecting the design and management of small craft, and of the precautions which are so absolutely necessary in the navigating of them.

But it must be distinctly understood that, in selecting this subject, I have had no intention whatever of advocating, or recommending, such voyages, or of underrating the risks which, under the most favourable circumstances, they involve ; my purpose has simply been to combine a little information with, I hope, a great deal of interest and amusement; and if my book serves but to while pleasantly away an idle hour or two for the general reader, or conveys a scrap of useful information to the young yachtsman, that purpose will be fully accomplished.

HARRY COLLINGWOOD.

October, 1878.

B

CONTENTS OF VOL. I.

The Secret of the Sands.

CHAPTER I.

THE WRECK.

_ _ was the last week in the month of November, 18—, when the event occurred which proved to be the *primum mobile* of the following adventures.

The weather, for some days previous, had been unusually boisterous for the time of year, and had culminated, on the morning on which my story opens, in a "November gale" from the south-west, exceeding in violence any previous gale within the memory of "the oldest inhabitant" of the locality. This is saying a great deal, for I was at the time living in Weymouth, a most delightful summer resort, where, however, the feelings are likely to be more or less harrowed every winter by fearful

VOL. I.   1 wrecks on the far-famed and much-dreaded Chesil Beach, which connects the mis-named *island* of Portland with the mainland.

We had dined, as usual, at the primitive hour of one o'clock; and with Bob Trunnion—about whom I shall have more to say anon—I had turned out under the verandah to enjoy our post-prandial smoke, according to invariable usage. My sister Ada would not permit us the indulgence of that luxury indoors, and no conceivable disturbance of the elements could compel us to forego it altogether.

We were pacing the verandah side by side, quarter-deck fashion, with our hands behind our backs and our weeds between our teeth, making an occasional remark about the weather as the sheeted rain swept past us, and the trees in the distance and the leaf-denuded shrubs in the garden bowed before the fury of the blast, when a coastguardman, whom I had occasionally encountered and spoken to in my rambles, came running past, enveloped in oilskins and topped by a sou-wester.

As he went by, seeing us, he shouted, "Ship

coming ashore in the West Bay, sir!" and was the next minute at the bottom of the hill, *en route*, as fast as his legs could carry him, for the town.

Our house was situated in a pleasant suburb called Rodwell; the high-road which passed our door led direct to the Smallmouth Sands, at the farther extremity of which was the Chesil Beach; and we conjectured that the coastguardman had come from the beach along this road to give notice to the chief officer stationed in the town.

To run indoors, don our foul-weather rigging, and notify my sister that we were off to the scene of the anticipated wreck, was the work of a moment. The next we were in the road, inclined forward at an angle of forty-five degrees against the wind, and staggering slowly ahead in the direction of the sands. The coastguardman had a fair wind of it, and was going a good eight knots when he passed us; but just at the top of the hill, as we were exposed to the full strength of the gale, we did not forge ahead at more than about one knot. However, matters mended soon after, for we surmounted the brow of the hill, and began the descent on the opposite side; here the road took a slight bend, which brought the wind well abeam; so keeping close under the hedge to windward of us, we rattled away as fast as we could go.

After nearly an hour's severe exertion we reached the beach. The vessel which was expected to come on shore was a full-rigged ship, apparently of about eight hundred or a thousand tons, and evidently a foreigner, by her build and rig. Some conjectured her to be French, some Spanish, and others avowed their belief that she was a German; but she was still too far off, and the weather too thick, to enable any one to form a clear judgment as to her nationality.

"Whoever she is," said the chief boatman, "the skipper of her is a downright good seaman, and doesn't intend to lose his ship whilst he can do anything to save her. He drove into the bay about two hours ago, sir," said he, turning to me, "and this is the second time that he's tried to fetch out again; but, Lord! he don't know this place so well as I do, or he'd be as sartain as I be that she'll never go outside o' the Bill o' Portland again. The ship don't float that, with her sails alone, could get out of the bay, once she got into it, with the wind and tide the way it is now; and afore the tide turns he'll be knocked into match-wood, or my name's not Joe Grummet. There he comes round again," continued the man, who had kept his eye on the vessel all the time he was speaking; "but it's no good; he's more 'n a mile to leeward of where he fetched last time, and he'd better give it up and run her ashore whilst 'tis light enough to get the hands out of her, if so be as it please God to let any on 'em come ashore alive."

The vessel had, as Grummet remarked, altered her course; running off rapidly before the wind, and consequently towards the land; and those who knew nothing about nautical matters would have supposed that her commander had at length given up the contest, and was about to run her on shore.

But we knew better. The vessel had merely been kept away in order to *wear* her; *staying* in such a tremendous gale and sea being utterly out of the question. And as we watched we saw her come slowly to the wind on the opposite tack;

her yards were braced sharp up, her sheets flattened in, and once more the battle for life was
resumed against the hostile elements.

But it was evident that the noble ship's career
was ended. The operation of *wearing* had
brought her into fearful proximity with the land;
and though she carried reefed mainsail and foresail
under close reefed topsails, and fore and main topmast staysails, it was evident that she was driving
to leeward at a frightful rate, and that the period of
her existence must now be measured in minutes.

"Now, lads! bear a hand!" shouted Grummet,
"and let's signal her to run in here. The beach
is steeper here than anywhere within the next
three or four mile; and if he happens to come in
on the back of a sea, he'll run up pretty near high
and dry; and we may get some of the poor souls
ashore alive, and cheat Davy Jones out of the best
part of his bargain this bout, anyway."

A large red bandana handkerchief was produced
and seized to the end of a boat-hook; this extem-
pore flag and staff Grummet took in his hand, and,
proceeding to the summit of the beach, commenced
waving it to and fro, to attract the attention of the

people on board the doomed ship. She was now so close that we could see the two men at her wheel, and a man, whom we supposed to be the master, standing by the mizen rigging.

Just abaft the mainmast, and huddled together under the shelter of the weather bulwarks, we could see some seven or eight more of her crew, and others were doubtless cowering elsewhere out of sight.

Grummet waved his flag energetically from the crest of the beach, and the coastguardmen busied themselves in making such slight preparations as were in their power to assist the crew in escaping from the wreck. Several coils of line had been brought down to the beach; one man who announced himself to be a good swimmer, had secured an end of the smallest of these to his waist; he now stood prepared to divest himself of all his superfluous clothing at a moment's notice, and to attempt the hazardous experiment of rushing into the boiling surf, to drag out any poor unfortunate whom he might be able to reach. Others were engaged in various ways in preparing themselves to render what assistance was in their power, when a cry from Grummet announced that the crisis had arrived; on looking up we saw that the stranger's fore topmast had gone in the cap; and now hung to leeward, with the topsail and topmast staysail thrashing to ribbons; the latter threatening at every jerk to take the bowsprit out of the ship. The foresail was also split from head to foot; and, even as we looked, the overstrained canvas gave way, and, fluttering for a moment in the furious gale, parted from the bolt-ropes, and came flying like a shred of cloud to leeward.

The ship, thus deprived of her head-sail, luffed into the wind; and the moment that the rest of her canvas shook, away it came also, leaving her helpless and unmanageable, with the sea sweeping her deck fore and aft.

"Now stand by, men," shouted Grummet, "and each one do his best for the poor souls; for they were never nearer to death's door than they will be in another two minutes. If he had run her stem on to the beach they might have stood a chance; but I fear it is all over with them now, for she'll come ashore broadside on, and all on us knows what that means."

Fortunately, the catastrophe had happened immediately to windward of that part of the beach on which we stood; a spot, as Grummet had observed, where the shipwrecked crew would have a better chance of reaching the shore alive than they would have had if stranded on any other part of it for some miles on either side ; but the loss of their sails had rendered the prospect of their escape considerably less than it would have been had they been able to watch their chance, *sail* the ship in on the crest of a wave, and so beach her.

The next half minute or so was one of most intense and painful excitement to us spectators on shore. Each man moved nearer to the water, and cast off some article of clothing, or gave a last look to the line, or a final adjustment to the life-buoy round his waist. For myself, I had stripped off my jacket and waistcoat, and placed them, together with my hat, in the hands of my friend Bob, who could not swim ; and I now stood with the end of a line, knotted into a bowline, in my hand, ready to do anything which the emergency of the moment might require.

The master of the vessel appeared to be aware of our intention, and the meaning of the signal which Grummet had shown; and as it was now impossible to run the ship *stem* on upon the beach, he did the next best thing; and waving his hand to the men who, like true seamen, still stuck to the wheel, they put the helm hard up, that she might come in stern on.

The manœuvre was partially successful; but unfortunately she came ashore between two seas; and the undertow of the one taking her stern, whilst the succeeding sea struck her bow, she fell broadside to in an instant, her three masts went by the board, and the sea made a clean breach over her.

One poor fellow was seen to leap overboard at the moment that the ship struck; and half-a-dozen of the men on the beach rushed down into the water, making frantic efforts to get at him. But he could not swim; and those who tried to reach him were flung back, bruised and senseless, upon the beach, only to be dragged away again as the sea receded; and had it not been for the ropes and life-buoys round their waists, by which their comrades hauled them on shore, they must have lost their lives. As it was, one of them, in some way or other, got out of the life-buoy, and we saw him swept away almost from our very feet.

I was an expert swimmer; and as soon as I saw the poor fellow being swept away, I slipped my head and shoulders through the bowline knot I held in my hand, dashed into the surf, and, resorting to my usual tactics of diving through the breakers, managed to get hold of the man with one hand, while I raised the other above my head, as a signal to those on shore to haul away upon their end of the line.

As soon as I felt the line tighten round me, I grasped the man round the body, and in another moment we were both on the beach, in the arms of those who had run down to meet us. By these we were dragged up out of reach of the sea, and, on staggering to my feet, I had the satisfaction of seeing the man who had jumped overboard from the wreck being hauled on board again.

Loud were the thanks and praises I received for my conduct in bringing the other on shore;

but without waiting to listen to them, I hastily explained that I would try to take a line on board the wreck, as, if I could succeed in this, there might possibly be some chance of saving the major portion, if not the whole of the crew. Accordingly I dashed into the surf once more; and at length, after the most superhuman efforts, though the distance was barely thirty yards, I reached the ship's side, and was drawn on board by a line which her crew threw to me. The men crowded round me, rapidly talking in some language which I could not understand, and looking as much relieved as though I had the power of taking them all on my back at once, and swimming on shore with them. I stood for a moment to recover my breath; and at the same time looked about to see what resources might be at my command. I noticed a towing hawser coiled away upon what had originally been the deckhouse forward, but which was now stove in and battered almost out of recognition. An eye was spliced in one end of this hawser; and taking it up, I signed to the men to pass it over the stump of the foremast.

They understood me, and, seeing my object in wishing it done, they had it over in a twinkling; in another moment, they had the heavy coil capsized, the other end bent on to the line which I had brought on board with me, and were paying it rapidly over the side.

As I turned to address the master of the vessel, who, I noticed as I was hauled up the side, was then standing at the break of the poop, issuing instructions to his crew, I saw him in the act of descending the poop-ladder, and I stepped towards him. At this moment the ship was lifted up by a perfect mountain of a sea, and hove over on her beam-ends; all hands of us were flung violently to leeward; and before apparently any of us had time to recover our feet, another sea swept down upon us; there was a terrific—an ear-splitting crash, a wild, agonised cry, and I found myself clear of the wreck, struggling wildly for life, with the body of the master within arm's length of me.

He was apparently dead, and floating face downwards; but I grasped him by the hair, turned him on his back, and struck out for the beach. Twice were we flung like corks upon the pebbles of the strand, and twice dragged off into deep water again by the merciless undertow. The first time I dug my fingers, knees, and the toes of my boots into the pebbles, in the hope of bringing myself and my senseless charge to an anchor; but I might as well have attempted to grasp the air. The whole of that portion of the beach which was exposed to the action of the sea was a vast moving mass, the shingle being alternately thrown up and sucked back again in tons, as the water hurled itself high upon the beach and then rushed back into the foaming abyss.

The second time we were thrown up with such violence that I was stunned; but the third time the brave fellows on the beach, who had been making the most frantic efforts to get at us, would take no denial. They watched their chance, and as they saw us again drifting in, two, with ropes round their waists, rushed into the sea, grasped us, one each, firmly round the body; and, though they were lifted off their feet and dragged away to seaward like feathers by the retiring breaker, never let go their hold until we were hauled up high and dry, clear beyond the reach of the heaviest wave.

The efforts made to restore me to consciousness were soon successful, but my fellow-sufferer, the master of the vessel, appeared to be seriously injured. It was nearly half an hour before the faintest signs of returning animation were perceived; and when at length consciousness returned, the poor fellow appeared to be suffering the most excruciating agony.

As soon as I was once more able to look about me, I found that the wave which had washed the master and me overboard, had broken the wreck in two just abaft the mainmast, flinging the stern portion much nearer the shore, whilst it had turned the other half fairly bottom up, precipitating, of course, all the poor fellows, who were so busy paying out the hawser, into the sea. The people on the beach watched eagerly for their reappearance above water, but not one of them was ever seen again. It afterwards transpired that there was not a swimmer amongst the entire crew, which, all told, amounted to fifteen hands.

The intelligence of a wreck had attracted a large concourse of people to the spot, notwithstanding the discomfort attendant on being abroad in so violent a gale; and one gentleman had taken upon himself to despatch omnibuses from the town, well supplied with blankets, etc., for the relief and benefit of any poor sufferers who might reach the shore alive. Into one of these vehicles the unfortunate master of the ship was now placed with the utmost care, a couch being extemporised for him in the bottom of the 'bus by piling together all the blankets which had been sent. In spite, however, of the utmost care in driving, the jolts were frequent, and sometimes rather heavy, and the poor fellow's groans indicated such intensity of suffering, that by the time we were half way to town I decided I would take him to my own house, whereby he would be spared nearly half an hour of anguish.

It fortunately happened that, just as I had come to this resolution, a gentleman rode up, and learning who we had inside, volunteered his services. I immediately accepted them, desiring him to ride back to the town, and despatch to my house the ablest physician he could find. When the 'bus drew up at our door, the doctor was there in readiness for his patient, whom we lifted out, apparently in the last stage of exhaustion, and carried carefully into the house and upstairs into my own room, where my sister (advertised by Bob, who had made the best of his way home on foot) had a cheerful fire blazing in the grate, hot water in abundance, and everything else ready that her womanly sympathy could suggest.

CHAPTER II.

THE SECRET.

THE doctor remained with the sick man more than half an hour; and when I heard his footstep descending the staircase I went out and met him.

"The poor fellow is sinking rapidly," said he, in reply to my inquiries; "he has received severe internal injuries, and is bleeding to death inwardly. I can do nothing, absolutely *nothing* for him. Keep him quiet, and humour him as much as you can; excitement of any kind will only hasten his dissolution." I cheerfully promised to do all I could for the dying man; and the doctor took his leave, promising to call again the last thing in the evening.

As soon as the doctor was out of the house I went upstairs and into the sick-room, where I found the patient in bed, and Bob, with his boots off, gliding as quietly about the room as a trained hospital nurse, doing all he could to contribute to the comfort of his charge.

The opening of the door attracted the sick man's attention, and he feebly turned his head in my direction. As soon as he recognised me, he beckoned me to approach ; and I drew a chair to the side of the bed, asking him how he felt.

"Like one whose moments are numbered ;" replied he in perfectly pure English, but with a sonorous ring in the articulation of the words, which betrayed the fact that he was not speaking in his mother tongue. "Señor," he continued, "I am dying; the doctor has candidly told me so, though I needed no such assurance from him. The dreadful pangs which shoot through my tortured frame, are such as no man could long endure and live. I am a true Catholic, señor, and I would fain see a priest, or some good man of my own creed ; that I may confess, and clear my guilty soul from the stains which a life of sinful indulgence and contempt of Heaven's laws has polluted it with. I know there are many of

2—2

my faith in England, it may be that there are some in this place. Know you of any such?"

I replied that there certainly was a Catholic church in the town, but it was situated at some distance from the house in which he now lay; consequently it would perhaps be an hour before the priest could be found and brought to him; "but," added I, "I will send for him forthwith, and until he arrive I will sit here and keep you company."

So saying, I called Bob on one side, and directed him to proceed, as quickly as possible, into town, and bring the Reverend Father without a moment's delay, to the house.

As soon as Bob had departed, I resumed my seat by the bedside. Extending his burning hand towards me, he clasped mine, and endeavoured to raise it to his lips. "Señor," said he, "since it is the will of God that I am to die, I can but bow to that will in submission; but I would I could have been spared for a few years to testify my gratitude to you for your brave and noble efforts in behalf of my crew and myself—my poor people, my poor people," he sobbed—"all, all lost!"

He was silent for nearly five minutes; and I took advantage of the opportunity to explain to him that what I had done was no more than any other Englishman would do if he had the power, under similar circumstances; that such conduct was thought nothing of among our nation; being regarded as simply a duty which each man owed to every other, in like circumstances of distress with his own.

"I know—I know," replied he, "the English are as generous as they are brave; but still I would I had it in my power to express my thanks otherwise than in words. But I am alone in the world which I am so soon to leave. Not one have I of my own name or blood to whom I can bequeath my debt of gratitude; and when my ship went to pieces to-day (she was my own property, señor), I became a beggar. I have not so much property left as will pay the expenses of my burial; and here I lie, indebted to a stranger, and that stranger a foreigner, for the shelter which covers my dying head, as I soon shall be for the coffin and the grave which await my lifeless clay."

I was beginning to say something, with the intention of diverting his mind from so painful a train of thought, when he interrupted me eagerly.

"And yet," continued he, "poor as I am, it is in my power to make you rich—ay, beyond the utmost scope of your imagination. And I will, I *will!* Why should I take this secret to the grave with me? In a few hours I shall be beyond the want of earthly riches, but you, señor, are young, and look forward to a long life; doubtless, like other men, you have already indulged in many a bright day-dream which the possession of wealth would go far to realise. Listen, gentil señor; I must be brief, for I feel that I have no time to lose. I have been shipwrecked once before. It is now nearly three years ago since I sailed from Valparaiso for Canton, whence we were to proceed to Bombay, and so home round the Cape of Good Hope. I was then chief mate. We met with nothing but calms for the first three weeks of our passage, after which the weather changed, and we had a succession of adverse gales until we were within fifteen degrees of the line. Here we were worse off than ever, for at one moment we were lying in a glassy calm, and perhaps in five minutes afterwards were under close-reefed canvas, or possibly bare poles. At length a furious squall threw the ship on her beam-ends, and we were compelled to cut away all three of her masts to save her from foundering. And then the squall settled down into a perfect hurricane, and we could do nothing but suffer the ship to drive dead before it. Near midnight we were flung violently to the deck by a tremendous shock. The ship was on shore, dashing her bottom out upon the rocks. And it was so dark, señor, that we were unable to see each other. Oh! the horror of that night; it is as fresh upon me now as it was at the moment that it happened."

The poor fellow's face was streaming with perspiration. I begged he would not distress himself by recalling such painful recollections, but in spite of my remonstrance he continued his story.

"The ship broke up beneath our feet, and I found myself swimming, I knew not where, in the midst of a quantity of floating wreck, to a piece of which I clung. I was surrounded on every side by breakers; but not far from me I could perceive, by the absence of the phosphorescence, that the water was smooth. I urged myself, and the plank to which I clung, in that direction, and soon reached the smooth water; after which I suffered myself to drift. The water was quite warm, and I experienced no inconvenience whatever from my immersion. After the lapse of perhaps an hour, possibly more, I felt the ground beneath my feet, and staggering out of the water, I flung myself upon the dry land, and, notwithstanding the howling of the wind and the roar of the breakers, I fell into a deep and dreamless sleep.

"When I awoke the sun was beating fiercely down upon my uncovered head; the sky was cloudless; and a calm had succeeded to the gale of the night before. I rose to my feet, and on looking about me, discovered that I had been cast upon one of those coral islands which so thickly stud some portions of the Pacific. I was—as I am now—the only one who escaped the wreck alive. The bodies of my shipmates lay scattered along the shore; and a long and arduous day was spent in burying them where they lay, in such shallow graves as I could scoop in the sand with the aid of a piece of splintered plank. The beach was strewed with wreckage which had been washed over the reef and into the smooth water; and I was overjoyed to find amongst this the long-boat, perfectly uninjured. In her I visited the scene of the wreck; and there, after diligent search, I found the means and a sufficiency of appropriate materials to enable me to fit her for a lengthened voyage.

" I was more than two months on the island before my preparations were complete, for life was very enjoyable in that delightful spot, and I felt in no hurry to get away. At length, whilst walking along the beach one evening, my attention was attracted to three or four pieces of old, worm-eaten, weather-worn timber, which I had often noticed before, projecting above the sand; and curiosity now impelled me to walk up to and examine them. A careful scrutiny revealed to me that they formed part of the framework of a ship; and I resolved that I would return the next day and ascertain whether what I saw was merely a detached piece of wreck, or whether the entire hull lay there embedded in the sand.

" The next morning I repaired to the spot, armed with a primitive substitute for a shovel, which I had contrived to manufacture, and an iron bolt, to serve the purpose of a crow-bar, which I had procured the previous night by burning it out of a piece of wreck. I had worked for perhaps an hour, when I reached some planking, which I immediately recognised as the deck of the ship. This I proceeded to clear of sand, uncovering the deck in an extending circle from the spot where I had first encountered it, until I had an area of about fifteen or sixteen feet laid bare. And now I met with a breach in the deck; so instead of clearing away further, I began to dig down again. I toiled thus for four days, señor; by which time I had discovered that the wreck was that of a small vessel, of perhaps one hundred and thirty tons (though, small as she was, she had been built with a full poop) ; that she was a very ancient craft indeed ; and that her cargo consisted of nothing but *gold*, señor, that is, with the solitary exception of a strong wooden box (which, even after so long an interment, offered considerable resistance to my efforts to open it), containing an assortment of what

I took to be pebbles of different kinds, but which I afterwards found were unpolished gems. Yes, señor; there lay the gold in ingots, each wrapped in matting, and each ingot as much in weight as I could well lift. The matting was decayed in the first three or four tiers, and the metal discoloured almost to blackness; but towards the centre of the cargo (which is, probably, not more than twelve tiers deep altogether), the matting, though so rotten that it crumbled to dust as I touched it, had preserved the colour of the metal; and there it lay, bar after bar, gleaming with the dull yellow lustre peculiar to virgin gold.

"I ballasted my boat entirely with ingots; selecting the most discoloured I could reach, so that they might be less easily recognisable as gold, and the risk I ran of being ultimately robbed of them reduced in the same proportion. I also took a few of the pebbles (as I thought them) out of the box; after which I set to work to cover in the whole once more. I completed my task by burning down the timbers which had at first attracted my attention (and which I found were a portion of her stern frame), so that nothing remained above the surface of the sand to betray the whereabouts of my treasure. I then carefully marked the spot in such a manner that I could find it again ; and completed my preparations for departure with all speed.

" I had been at sea ten days, when I was taken ill. Whether it was the effect of excitement or exposure I know not ; but I fell into a raging fever, which left me almost at the point of death. I was so weak that I had not strength to crawl to the water-cask ; and the feeble efforts I made to reach it so exhausted me that at length I fell in a swoon to the bottom of the boat. In this condition I was discovered by a passing ship, the crew of which took me on board ; but, as a smart breeze happened to be blowing at the time, they would not wait to hoist in my boat ; and she was set adrift with enough gold on board her to have purchased a principality.

" Regrets were useless, and the loss, heavy as it was, troubled me little ; I knew where to find sufficient to satisfy my utmost needs. At length I reached home, and, by the merest accident, bethought myself one day of my pebbles. I suspected they were valuable, or they would not have been found where they were. Judge of my surprise when I learned that the four I had left (for I lost the rest somewhere) were worth a sufficient sum to enable me to do exactly what I wished; viz., buy a ship of my own. I did so; and was on my way in her to my treasure-island, when the gale sprung up which has reduced me to my present condition.

"And now, señor, I am about to put *you* in possession of such information as will enable you to find my island. It is in latitude about — S., and in longitude about — W., as nearly as I had the means of ascertaining; and is uninhabited, and, I should say, unknown; for during my entire stay there, I never observed one solitary sign of man's foot having ever pressed the soil. You will readily recognise the island from the fact that it has a remarkable isolated group of seven cocoa-nut trees growing closely together on the extreme northernmost point of the island. The central tree of this group, and one of the others, bears a mark (made by the removal of a piece of bark) as large as a man's two hands. When you have identified these trees, walk away from them, keeping them *in one*, until you open, clear of the trees on the southern end of the island, a portion of the reef which you will observe just rising above the water's edge. When you have done this, you will be standing, as nearly as possible, immediately above the hole in the deck of the wreck, through which I burrowed to her golden cargo."

The Spaniard (for such I found him to be) then went on to describe the manner in which I should find the passage through the reef into the lagoon, giving me as much information as he could from memory of the various dangers to be avoided. He had carefully prepared a chart of the channel before leaving the island; but this was on board the vessel he had just lost.

I could see that the excitement produced by so much talking was fearfully reducing his strength, and I more than once endeavoured to persuade him to postpone the completion of his narrative, but he was sensible that he had but a short time to live, and so anxious was he to give me all the information necessary to enable me to discover

this strangely buried treasure, that my endeavour
to stop him did more harm even than the talking,
so I was compelled perforce to suffer him to
proceed. And though I felt it my duty to urge
him not to excite himself, I must confess that I
was deeply interested to learn how I might
become possessed of the wealth to which he
had referred in such glowing terms; for since it
was manifest that he could not live to enjoy it
himself, and as he had declared he had no
relative in the world, I thought I might as well
become his heir.

He continued to talk for some time longer, until
he had explained to me everything he could think
of which would facilitate my efforts to reach the
buried treasure; and then, with a sigh of mingled
exhaustion and relief, he closed his eyes, and
seemed to sink into a half sleep, from which he
roused himself at frequent intervals, to crave the
refreshment of a draught of lemonade.

At length the sound of carriage wheels was
heard; and almost immediately afterwards Bob
returned, accompanied by the Catholic priest. The
sick man opened his eyes, and feebly welcomed

the good old man who had so readily answered his appeal for spiritual consolation. I then retired, leaving them alone to engage in the most solemn rite appertaining to their religion.

Rather more than an hour elapsed before I was recalled to the sick-room. When I stood once more at the bedside of the dying Spaniard, I saw that he had but a few minutes longer to live. He was so weak, the clergyman said, that it was with the utmost difficulty he had succeeded in expressing his wish to see me again before he died.

As I drew near his eye brightened, and a faint smile of welcome lighted up his face. His lips moved, but so faint was the whisper which escaped them, that I was obliged to bow my face close to his ere I could distinguish the words. With a painful effort he gasped, " Señor, promise me that, if you succeed, you will have two hundred masses said for my soul ?"

When I assured him that his request should be faithfully complied with, the contracted brow relaxed; the expression of anxiety vanished; and in its place a smile of satisfaction and perfect happiness slowly spread itself over the pinched and pallid features, where, the next moment, it was indelibly fixed by the hand of death.

I have dwelt at such length upon this introductory episode of my story that I must now " turn the hands up and make sail" in earnest, for we have a voyage of many thousands of miles before us ; and, like all thorough seamen, having once shipped for the voyage, we are impatience personified until the anchor is atrip, the canvas sheeted home, the watch set, and the lively little barkie dashing merrily away over the heaving billows, her snowy canvas gleaming in the setting sun, and the cliffs of Old England fast fading into purple mist astern.

CHAPTER III.

AFTER we had reverently laid the Spaniard to rest in his alien grave, I gave my friend Bob a full and accurate account of all that had passed, showing him at the same time the copious notes I had, at the earliest opportunity, jotted down to assist and refresh my memory in case I should ever find myself in a position to seek the hidden treasure.

But it is now necessary that I should introduce the *dramatis personæ* who have already cast their shadows on the curtain ; and this I will do with all possible brevity.

"*Place aux dames.*" Ada Collingwood, my darling and only sister, was at this time approaching her seventeenth year, and was a dainty specimen of lovely girlhood just budding into still lovelier womanhood. Her figure was petite, promising in due time to develope into the most fault-less perfection of shape : and her laughing blue eyes and rich profusion of silky golden hair set off to perfection a face which, perhaps, no one would have dreamed of calling *beautiful*, any more than they would have dreamed of denying that it was charmingly piquant, and irresistibly *pretty*. Her temper was equable ; she was gifted with a rich flow of animal spirits, and a keen perception of the ludicrous, which would have upset the gravity of the most confirmed hypochondriac.

Nevertheless, if occasion required it, her merry ringing laugh could be hushed, her joyous elasticity of movement could be subdued, and no one better than she could assume the *rôle* of the sick-nurse, or the tender and sympathising confidante of distress. And lastly, she adored, with a blind unreasoning idolatry for which there was no excuse, your humble servant, her unworthy brother.

Of myself, it becomes me not to say very much. I was just turned twenty-one : six feet high : and vanity whispered, in confirmation of my sister's energetic and oft-repeated assertions, a trifle more than moderately good-looking. I was an only son (as my sister was an only daughter), and I had received my education at the Royal Naval School at Greenwich, with the understanding that I was to join my father on its completion, when he would continue and finish what is there so well begun, thus making me "every inch a sailor."

On leaving school I joined my father (who was master and part owner of a fine dashing clipper), in the capacity of midshipman, and went some six or seven voyages with him : on the last of which, or rather a few days after its termination, I was seized with a violent attack of rheumatic fever, from which I had not recovered sufficiently to re-join the ship by the time that she was once more ready for sea. I was consequently left at home under Ada's care (my dear mother had been dead some years), to recover at leisure, and amuse myself as well as I could, until another voyage should be accomplished, and an opportunity once more offered for me to repossess myself of my quarters in the old familiar berth. That opportunity never arrived, for at the time my story opens, my father had been two years "missing." He sailed from Canton with the first cargo of the new season's teas, and from the moment that the good ship disappeared seaward she had never been heard of; not the faintest trace of a clue to the mystery of her fate having, so far, been discovered.

Bob Trunnion was a middle-aged man, of medium stature, great personal strength, and no very marked pretensions to beauty; but he was as thorough an old sea-dog as ever looked upon salt water. His visage was burnt to a deep brick-red by years of exposure to all sorts of weather; and his hair and beard, which had once been brown, were now changed to the hue of old oakum by the same process, except where, here and there, a slight sprinkling of grey discovered itself. He had been a sailor almost all his life; having "crept in through the hawse-pipe" when he was only twelve years old; since when, by close application and perseverance, he had gradually worked his way aft to the quarter-deck. He joined my father's ship as second mate, on the same voyage as I did, and on the following voyage took the chief mate's berth, in place of a man whom my father was compelled to discharge for confirmed drunken-ness.

The last time that my poor father passed down Channel, outward bound, Bob had the misfortune (as we thought it then), to fall off the poop and break his arm.   It was what the surgeons call a compound fracture, and certainly looked to be a very ugly one; so, as the ship happened at the time to be off St. Alban's Head, my father ran into Weymouth roads, and sent Bob ashore to our house to be cured, and to bear me company; ship-ping in his stead the second mate, and picking up a new second mate somewhere about the town.

Thus it happened that Bob and I, old shipmates as we were, happened to be both away from our ship when her mysterious fate overtook her.   As soon as we were both recovered, we sought and obtained berths, always in the same ship, for short voyages; returning home about once in every six weeks or two months, with the hope of hearing either that my father had returned, or that some news had arrived of him.   For the last twelve months we had abandoned the former hope, but the latter would probably be many years before it finally took its flight.

This introduction and explanation are necessary to the understanding of what is to follow; and now, having fairly weathered them both, we may take up the thread of the story, and follow it out to the end without further interruption.

I have already said that I took an early opportunity to give Bob a detailed account of the Spaniard's revelation to me. This was on the evening of the day on which we laid the poor fellow in his grave; and I told my story while we and my sister were seated comfortably round the fire after tea, with the curtains drawn close, and everything made snug for the night.

Bob listened with the utmost attention to my story (as did also my sister), occasionally requesting me to "say that ag'in," as some point in the narrative was reached which he wished to bear particularly in mind; and when I had finished he sat for some time staring meditatively between the bars of the grate.

At length, " Well, Harry, my lad, what do you intend to do ?" said he.

" That," replied I, " is just the point upon which I want your advice. If this story be true——"

" No fear about that," said Bob. " It's true enough. The thing's as plain and circumstantial as the ship's course when it's pricked off upon the chart. There ain't a kink in the yarn from end to end ; it's all coiled down as neat and snug as a new hawser in the ropemaker's yard ; and besides, dyin' men don't spin yarns with no truth in 'em, just for divarsion's sake like."

" Well," said I, " I am disposed, with you, to think that the story *is* quite true ; the man could have no object in telling it if it were not so. The question is, what is to be done in the matter ?"

" Done !" exclaimed Ada, " why, what *should* be done, Harry, except that you go to this island, dig up the gold, bring it home, and live like a gentleman ever afterwards ?"

This was Ada's great ambition ; that I should be placed in the position of a gentleman. She had a theory—whence derived I know not—that it was my destiny to become a man of unbounded means; and that my life was to be passed in an atmosphere of splendour and luxury only equalled by that enjoyed by the most favoured heroes of the "Arabian Nights." And this was an entirely disinterested feeling on her part too; for though she would often laughingly prophesy what would happen "when I should become a rich man," I never knew her to utter a word which suggested the idea that *she* would in any way be a gainer by my acquisition of wealth.

"More easily said than done, pet," replied I, patting her soft cheek. "What is to become of you whilst I am gone?"

"Why, I shall stay here with Mrs. Moseley (our housekeeper) until your return, and be the first to welcome you back," said she.

"Well," replied I, "I think suitable arrangements for your comfort and safety could be made without much difficulty; but," said I, appealing to Bob, "how is this gold to be got at and brought home in safety? I have not the means of purchasing a ship of my own; and if I had, do you think it would be safe to trust so much treasure with a crew, picked up though ever so carefully?"

" Ah ! now you 'pawls me," replied Bob, rubbing the back of his head reflectively. " I've sailed with crews as you might ha' trusted with untold gold, at least I've thowt so at the time I was with 'em ; but mayhap, if temptation was throwed in their way, they mightn't be able to stand out agin it ; there's no gettin' to the bottom o' the heart o' man. As to the ship, that's easy enough. If you ain't got the cash to *buy*, you can always *charter*."

" True," said I, "and if I could *make sure* of finding a sufficient number of thorough good men, that is the course I should be inclined to pursue. Do you think, Bob, that by diligent search we could find some six or eight really reliable men ? The craft need not be a large one, you know——"

" There you've hit the solution of the enigmy, as the schoolmaster said," replied Bob, bringing his clenched fist down upon my knee with an emphasis which impressed me for the remainder of the evening : " How much of that gold now do you reckon would make your fortune, lad ? you're pretty good at figures ; just cipher it up and let's hear ?"

" How much !" exclaimed I ; " oh, a very small

portion of the whole cargo would satisfy me if I had it here at this moment."

" How much ?" persisted Bob. " Would a *ton* of it be enough for you, boy ?"

" Yes, indeed," laughed I ; " a ton of pure gold —why, what do you suppose that would be worth, Bob ?"

" Hain't much of a idee," replied he.

" A ton of pure gold," said I, " is worth over one hundred thousand pounds, Bob ; I believe one hundred and twenty-five thousand pounds is nearer it's value ; though I cannot say for certain."

" Then," said Bob, " if we can manage to get, say, a couple of tons of it home, you will be satis-fied—eh ?"

" Perfectly," I replied ; " but how do you pro-pose to accomplish this ?" for I saw he had a scheme to bring forward.

" Nothing easier," replied Bob. " Build a little craft big enough to accommodate the two of us ; with room to stow away our grub and water, and the two tons of gold ; and up anchor and away."

" But," said I, " you forget that this island is somewhere in the Pacific. Such a craft as you speak of would be totally unfit for the voyage we contemplate."

" Why ?" inquired Bob.

" Why ?" repeated I, astonished at the question. " Simply because we should never get across the Bay of Biscay in her, to say nothing of the remainder of the voyage."

" Why not ?" demanded Bob, rather pugnaciously.

" Do you mean to say," I retorted, " that you can sit there and propose in cold blood such a hair-brained scheme as that we two should undertake a voyage to the Pacific in a mere *boat?*"

" I do," replied Bob emphatically. " That's a simple way out of all your difficulties. The craft will be your own ; there will be no risk of the crew rising upon us for the sake of our cargo ; and nobody to say ' What are we doing here ?' or ' What do you want there ?' Why, it will be a mere pleasure trip from end to end, all play and no work, leastways none to speak on !"

" But, my dear fellow, *do* be serious," protested I. " You know, as well as I do, that we should be swamped the first time we fell in with a capful of wind."

" Maybe we should, if we went to work like a couple of know-nothing land-lubbers," retorted Bob ; " but if we went to work like seamen, as we are, I should like to know what's to purvent our sailing round the world if we like ! Answer me that."

" Come, Bob, old man, let us hear the full extent of your proposition," said I. " I know that, whatever it may be, it will be the proposal of a thorough seaman, for if any one could carry out the wild scheme you have suggested, you are the man."

" 'Tain't such a very wild scheme neither," replied Bob. " Answer me this. How many people was saved from the *London* when she foundered in the Bay of Biscay ?"

" Nineteen, if I remember rightly," replied I.

" Very well ; now if a small boat of about twenty-five feet long or thereabouts, *open*, mind you, from stem to starn, could live twenty hours with nineteen people in her, as the *London's* pinnace did, in weather that the old ship herself couldn't stand up agin, how long will a full-decked boat of, say, thirty to thirty-five feet long, carefully constructed, and in good trim, live with only two men in her ?   And warn't I," continued he, " nineteen days *alone* in an open boat in the South Atlantic ; and didn't I make a v'y'ge of a thousand miles in her afore I struck soundings at St. Helena ?"

This last question referred to an adventure which had befallen Bob in his younger days, on an occasion when he had been cruelly deserted in a sinking ship by the rest of the crew, and had made his escape, as described by himself, after enduring unheard-of suffering.

" Then," questioned I, " you seriously entertain the belief that the scheme you have suggested is practicable ?"

" With ease and comfort," replied Bob.   " Now 'look here, Harry.   You can afford to build a craft such as I have described, and fit her out for the v'y'ge and still leave money enough at home to keep sauce-box here " (indicating Ada, who was to him as the apple of his eye) " comfortable and happy like till we come back.   You've a rare eye for a

sea-boat, and mine ain't bad, for that matter;
let's draught her out ourselves, since it's our own
lives as we are going to trust in her; and if we
don't turn out, between us, as pretty a sea-boat
as ever floated, why, turn to and lay me up in
ordinary for the rest of my days for a useless old
hulk, that's all. A boat thirty feet long, decked
all over, and carefully designed, *can't* sink, boy,
because we can easily arrange matters so as to
keep her dry inside; she'll ride as light as a gull
and as dry as a bone when big ships is making bad
weather of it, and as for the matter of capsizing,
bein' run down, or cast away, why they're dangers
as we are liable to in any ship, and must be
guarded against in every craft, large or small; and
our little barkie would carry comfortable all we
should want for the v'y'ge, for we could touch
here and there out and home to make good
deficiencies, and we two are men enough to
handle her in all weathers. Rig her as a cutter,
boy. I was once't aboard a cutter yacht in a trip
up the Mediterranean, and you've no idea what a
handy rig it is, once you're used to it. And the
way them cutters 'll hug the wind—why 't would

make a difference of nigh on a couple of thousand miles, out and home, in the length of the
passage."

I began to be infected with Bob's enthusiasm.
The scheme, which had at first appeared to me
as the very acme of fool-hardiness, now, under
the influence of Bob's eloquence, gradually assumed an appearance of reasonableness, and a
promising prospect of success, which was very
fascinating.   Nevertheless, I could not but remember that the proposed voyage would take us
into latitudes subject to the most frightful and
sudden tempests, and I could not help thinking
(as I pointed out to Bob) that our cockle-shell
would stand but a poor chance in a cyclone or a
black squall.

"Look here, Harry, my boy," remarked Bob
gravely, "as I propose to ship on this here
v'y'ge as chief mate, I ain't likely to forget that
there's such dangers as them you've just mentioned.   But suppose you was to cork up a
bottle, or clap the lid on an empty biscuit-tin, and
heave 'em overboard, do you think they'd live
through one or t'other ?   In course they would,

because salt water can't get inside of 'em, and as long as they keep dry holds they'll float, let the weather be what it will, and so 'll our craft, for the same reason. And when the weather's too bad to sail the barkie, we can heave her to, and when it's too bad for that we can *anchor* her, my boy, go below, slide on the top of the companion, and turn in until the weather clears up."

" But," said I, " we cannot anchor in the middle of the Atlantic. Suppose we should be caught in a cyclone there, for instance ?"

" We *can* anchor *there*, lad, with a *floating* anchor, which will keep her head to wind; and with everything snug aloft and on deck, and a floating anchor ahead with about sixty fathoms of cable veered out, she would ride out *in safety* any gale that ever blew out of the heavens."

This last remark closed the case, and secured a verdict for the defendant. I *knew* that every word Bob spoke was literally true, and the audacity of the enterprise so fascinated me that I resolved on the spot to undertake it, if it should be found, on going into details, that a craft, capable of being handled by our two selves, could stow away, without being overloaded, such provisions, etc., as we should need for the voyage.

The following morning, immediately after breakfast, I got out my drawing-board, strained a sheet of paper upon it, and, with Bob at my side to give me the benefit of his opinion upon every line I traced upon the paper, set to in earnest to design the little craft in which we proposed to embark on our adventurous voyage.

Before putting a line upon paper, however, we settled the plan of her internal arrangements. It was our intention to make her lines as fine as her respective dimensions would permit; she was to be, in fact, a small *yacht*. We knew that every vessel with sharp lines must necessarily be wet, unless the weights she would have to carry were all concentrated about her midship section, or broadest part, so we decided that as far as was practicable such should be the arrangement with us; and we knew that, if we could succeed in this, our barkie might be as sharp as we could make her, and still be dry and comfortable. We accord-

ingly prepared a list of our requirements, as far as
we could think of them, calculated the space they
and the ballast would occupy, and then roughly
sketched out the proposed lines. These were
altered, rearranged, and improved upon time
after time, until at length we felt we had got
them as near perfection as the dimensions of the
boat and our own knowledge would carry us.
And I may as well say at once that throughout
the entire voyage we never had the slightest
reason to think our little vessel could be in any
way improved upon by alteration.

It is not probable that so long a voyage as
ours will be often undertaken again in such a very
small craft as we accomplished it in ; but there are
many men, I have no doubt, who would gladly
receive a hint as to the most advantageous form
for a small boat in which they might safely adventure, alone, or with a friend, a cruise, say round
the British Isles, or across the Channel and along
the French coast; and therefore, as this story is
written for the amusement only of such people as
love boats, I think I may venture to trespass so
far on my readers' patience as to give such a hint

in the shape of a brief description of the *Water Lily*, as Ada christened her.

She was, then, thirty-six feet long, and twelve feet beam on the water-line ; but, in designing her midship section, we caused her sides to swell out boldly *above* water, so that her greatest beam was fourteen feet, at a point one foot six inches above the water-line.   At this point her side *tumbled home* two inches as it was carried upwards to her deck, and from the same point the side curved quickly inwards and downwards until it met the water-line, when it swept under water with an almost imperceptible curve for some distance, and then took a moderately quick bend downwards to meet her keel.   This gave us a vessel in shape very much like the centre-board model of boat, but with a deep keel, and consequently great lateral resistance, and space low down in the hull for the stowage of ballast.   We thus secured a *very* small displacement, a light buoyant hull, extraordinary stability, and a fair amount of *power*.

The hull was divided into three compartments by bulkheads with wide doors which, if necessary, we could close *water-tight*.   In the *fore* compartment we decided to place *nothing* except the smallest and lightest cooking-stove we could find. In the midship compartment it was intended to stow our ballast, water-tank, provisions, the chain cables, and in fact everything which we could possibly place there, leaving only a narrow passage amidships to pass to and fro. The after compartment we intended to make our cabin, and there we arranged also to sling our hammocks. It will easily be understood that there was not an inch of spare room anywhere; but as our lives would be spent almost entirely on deck, we did not mind that very much.

Having designed our craft, the next question was, who should build her? Bob was strongly in favour of having her built in the town, so that we might oversee the laying of every plank, and the driving of every nail; but I knew there were firms who could safely be trusted to honestly put the best of work and material into the little vessel without being watched; and I determined to put her into the hands of a very celebrated firm of London boat-builders.

Accordingly, Bob and I ran up to town, taking

my sister with us for a holiday, and on the morning after our arrival, having seen Ada safely disposed of for the day with some friends of ours, we two men set out for the building-yard.

I placed our design in the hands of the principal, telling him at the same time that we wanted a boat of those dimensions, and, if possible, built on those lines, and that she was intended to keep at sea in *all* weathers.

He looked rather surprised at the last stipulation ; but after carefully examining the drawing, and asking us our reasons for certain little peculiarities of shape, he confessed that, as far as his experience went, he could frankly say he had never seen a model better adapted for the purpose.

" And yet, gentlemen," said he, " she will be wonderfully fast, for, in the first place, her *hull* is of such a shape that it will offer but a trifling resistance to forward motion ; and, in the next place, these overhanging top-sides will give her such extraordinary stability, as soon as she begins to heel over, that you will be able to carry enormous sails."

We were very glad to hear our own judgment thus confirmed by a man, part of whose business it was to form a correct opinion with respect to the points upon which he had touched, and we said as much.

He took a great deal of interest in what must, after all, have been a very trifling matter to him; and both Bob and I had reason often afterwards to congratulate ourselves that we had confided the building of our boat to such good hands.

He proposed that she should be *composite* built; that is, that for the sake of lightness and strength combined, her frame should be of steel, with an inner skin of thin steel plate, and an outer planking of two thicknesses of mahogany. The ribs were to be arranged *diagonally*, crossing the keel at an angle of forty-five degrees, and intersecting each other at right angles, thus converting her entire frame into a sort of lattice-work girder.

It was arranged that all the fastenings of the inner thickness of planking should be of iron, whilst the outside planks should be secured with copper fastenings. The utmost care was exercised (and, as experience proved, with complete success) to prevent the slightest approach to galvanic action, and one of the precautions taken was, I remember well, the painting of the inner planking with melted india-rubber, which was laid on coat after coat until there was about one-sixteenth of an inch of the rubber between the outer and inner planks.

As we did not intend to sail until the following summer, the builder had about eight months in which to put our little ship together, a circumstance at which he expressed great satisfaction, as he said it would enable him to pick and choose his materials, and put careful work into her.

We arranged, at the same time, for the construction of a boat to take with us, as we felt that in the event of any untoward accident happening, we ought to have something to take to for the saving of our lives, and we knew also that there would be many occasions when we should require something to answer the purposes which a boat answers with regard to a ship.

The designing of this boat was beset by difficulties, all originating in one, viz., want of space in which to stow her. To think of carrying her on deck was out of the question, as the deck was not spacious enough, in the first place, to receive such a boat as we wanted ; and even had it been, there was no chance of its remaining there ; it would have been carried away by the first sea which swept over us. We required something large enough to carry us both, and a stock of provisions in addition, so that should it be necessary to abandon the *Water Lily*, we might hope to reach land, or fall in with a ship. We also wanted something that should be essentially a *life-boat*, whilst she should also be very fast. How to obtain all these desiderata, and at the same time overcome the difficulty in respect to room, we knew not. But, resolved not to be baffled, we set our wits to work, and at length schemed out a design of an exceedingly novel character, which proved in all respects a most brilliant success.

Two hollow steel cylinders, of very thin metal, twenty-six feet long and one foot diameter in the centre, tapering gradually away to nothing at each end, were constructed in thirteen lengths of two feet each. These lengths, being of different diameters, stowed one within the other, thus taking up very little room indeed. In either end of each length was inserted a narrow band of metal thick enough to allow of a worm and screw, so that all the lengths of each cylinder could be screwed together perfectly water-tight. A light steel framework of simple arrangement connected the two cylinders together, at a distance of six feet apart, with their centre lines parallel, and sup· ported, at a height of two feet above the top of the cylinders, a light stage ten feet long and six feet wide. On the top of the stage, and connected with the framework, was a step for a mast, and a gammon-iron for a bowsprit, and underneath the stage was a centre board which we could lower or raise at pleasure. A broad rudder, fixed to the after part of the stage, completed the design.

We spent a fortnight in London, and, having witnessed the laying of the *Water Lily's* keel, and inspected some of the timber which the builder proposed to use in her construction, I saw Ada safe home again, leaving Bob in London to look out for a ship, which, when I rejoined him a couple of days afterwards, he had found.

We shipped in her for a voyage to Constanti-
nople and Trebizond, which occupied us for eight
months, and when we returned to London, on the
termination of this voyage, we found the *Water
Lily* completed, with the exception of a few
finishing touches, which the workmen were then
giving her.

CHAPTER IV.

OUR TRIAL TRIP.

MR. WOOD (as we will call him, for the sake of giving the gentleman a name) took us into his office, and there laid before us a sail draught, which he had carefully prepared for the guidance of the sail-maker, in making the *Water Lily's* sails.

"You have never told me, gentlemen," said he, "*why* you are having this little craft built ; but the great pains which you have taken in the preparation of her design, and the whole tenour of your remarks when giving us the order to build her, impressed me at the time with a conviction that her destiny is to be something beyond that of most vessels of her size. As we proceeded with our work, I could not fail to be struck (as you will perhaps remember I was at my first glance at your drawing) with the fact, that whilst she is eminently calculated to prove a wonderfully fine little sea-boat, she is equally certain to develope most extraordinary sailing powers ; and so great is the interest I take in her that I could not be satisfied with intrusting the preparation of her sail draught to any other than myself; for I foresee that she will, in all probability, become a 'public character' so to speak, and in that capacity she will undoubtedly reflect great credit on her builders. I have there-fore calculated, with the utmost nicety, the pro-portion of her various sails, so that they may take effect to the greatest advantage ; and this is the result of my labours," producing at the same time the drawing to which I have referred.

I must confess that, for my own part, I was staggered at the enormous spread of canvas Mr. Wood proposed to pile upon our little boat ; but he declared that she would carry it with the greatest ease. " In fact," said he, " I have kept rather *within* the limit of her powers, bearing in mind a remark you made to the effect that she would have to keep to sea *in all weathers ;* and so confident am I that she is not over-sailed, that if you find I am wrong I undertake to bear all the expense of a new outfit of sails, and the necessary reduction of spars. With regard to your 'boat' (though to my mind she looks much more like an ingeniously designed *raft*), the idea is so new that I cannot take it upon myself to utter an opinion about her, though I can see no reason why she should not be as fast as she undoubtedly is safe."

We sent off the sail-drawing to Lapthorn of Gosport (determined to have the best made suit of sails it was possible to procure), with instructions to prepare them without delay, and then started off, by the first train, to Weymouth.

I found my dear sister safe and well, and more lovely than ever ; but her spirits were subdued by contemplation of the dangers attending the voyage upon which we were now so soon to embark. The poor girl had been thinking of little else it seemed during our absence, until the liveliest alarm had taken the place of that confidence with which she had viewed the expedition when it was first broached.

But Bob and I had talked matters over together in many a quiet night-watch, canvassing the various emergencies which might arise, and the best mode of meeting them ; and we were now confident that, with only the ordinary perils of the ocean to contend with, our adventure was not only feasible, but that it would certainly be crowned with success. And so we were well prepared to do battle with Ada's apprehensions, which we did so vigorously that we at length succeeded in restoring, in a great measure, the confidence she had lost.

We arranged, after a considerable amount of discussion, that our own house should be let, furnished as it was, during my absence, and that my sister should take up her quarters with an aunt who resided on the Esplanade, Mrs. Moseley accompanying her, with unlimited leave of absence from time to time to visit her own relatives.

These arrangements completed, Bob and I set out for London again, to superintend the rigging of our boat and to bring her round to Weymouth, from whence we intended to take our final departure.

On our arrival we found the little craft already in the water, with her mast stepped and her ballast (which was of lead, cast to fit the shape of her bottom) in. A portion of her ballast, consisting of a piece of lead weighing five hundredweight, was let into her keel about the midship section, and this, with two tons of lead inside, we thought would prove sufficient, after our "cargo" was stowed. Part of this cargo we intended to take from London with us, viz., the water-tank, filled, second suit of sails and flying-kites in the shape of spinnaker, jib-topsail, square-headed gaff-topsail, etc., also a four-pound rifle gun, with a stock of powder and shot, and a few percussion shells.

These we decided to take in case of our being obliged to assume a warlike attitude towards any savages we might come into contact with, as we had heard that the natives of some of the Pacific islands are particularly ferocious, and require to be dealt with promptly. We also provided ourselves with a couple of air-guns of improved construction and decidedly formidable character, four six-chambered revolving rifles, and the same number of revolver pistols, also a small but excellent chest of carpenter's tools, a medicine-chest, etc.

But when these and our boat were all stowed away, there still remained more room than I expected in our midship compartment, and the little craft floated with her load-line nearly a foot above the water's edge. I proposed ballasting her down to her proper depth with sand-bags, but Bob seemed anxious to test her sail-carrying powers light as she was, urging that though we should start well down in the water, she would lift as our provisions grew short ; and it was desirable to know by experiment beforehand how far we could lighten her with safety.

Our sails had arrived, and we proceeded to bend these forthwith, and set them ; as the weather being fine, with light air, a very favourable opportunity offered for stretching them gently and uniformly. We were as pleased with these sails as we were with the hull of our little craft. They were perfect masterpieces of the sailmaker's art, the jibs being angulated, and the mainsail, square-headed gaff-topsail, and trysail being made with gored cloths.

This latter arrangement was an extravagant one as to the amount of cloth used in the making of each sail, but we were more than repaid for it by the perfection of *set* in the sails, which stood as flat as boards. Our storm-sails were made of stout canvas, and the fine-weather ones of American cotton canvas, a most beautiful material, extremely light, yet so close woven that not a breath of the faintest breeze was lost, and they were white as snow.

Our standing rigging was of wire, this being lighter, and offering less windage than hemp-rigging of the same strength; but, in order to counteract its rigidity and give play to the spars, we adopted the expedient of connecting the dead-eyes to the chain-plates by a bolt and shackle arrangement, interposing a thick indiarubber-washer between the shackle and the bolt-head. This plan answered most admirably, and I would strongly recommend it to all users of wire-rigging. I am confident that, in a fresh breeze and a chopping sea, we gained fully a knot per hour in speed by it.

Whilst our sails were stretching, Bob and I occupied our time in looking about us for a few things which we thought we could better obtain

in London than anywhere else. Amongst these
was a couple of air mattresses for our hammocks,
which, when fully inflated, were capable of sustaining the weight of three men each in the water.
Another article was a cooking-stove, the smallest,
lightest, and most compact thing of the kind I
ever saw.

It had a boiler capable of heating a quart of
water, and an oven large enough to bake a fowl,
with kettle, saucepan, etc., for the top. The
grate proper was filled with fragments of some
substance, the name of which I have forgotten,
and underneath the grate was a sliding tray which
held a six-wicked lamp. The lamp being lighted
and placed in position, speedily raised the substance in the grate to a state of incandescence,
and there was our fire, which gave out a tremendous heat for the size of the grate. As an aid to
this stove, and an economiser of fuel, we purchased
also a most extraordinary invention, which was
named the "Norwegian cooking-stove" if I remember rightly.

This was not a stove at all, though it performed
the functions of one. It was simply a *box*, so con-

structed that it retained all the heat your dish might happen to contain when placed in it. The mode of operation was to place your fowl or pie, or what not, in the oven until it was thoroughly hot through, then take it out, place it in the " Norwegian," shut it up for two or three hours, take it out, and lo! your dinner was cooked to perfection. The fuel which this affair saved us during the voyage would have bought a dozen of them. We spent a week looking about for such things as these, and I am confident that, but for the economy of space which we were able to secure through the aid of these contrivances, our voyage must have come to a sudden and igno- minious conclusion.

At length we were all ataunto ; sails stretched to perfection and properly bent, our *impedimenta* all carefully and snugly stowed, and everything ready for a start. At the instigation and through the kindness of some yachting friends of mine, I had been introduced to and was elected a member of the Royal ——— Yacht Club ; so one fine morning towards the latter end of July we loosed our sails, set them, ran our Club burgee up to the mast-head and the ensign up to the peak, and made a start for Weymouth. At the last moment Mr. Wood, the builder of our little craft, came on board, saying that as he had nothing very pressing for the day, and was curious to see something of the way in which the *Water Lily* behaved, he would take a passage with us as far as Gravesend, if we had no objection.

We were only too pleased to have his company, and of course gave him a cordial welcome. The moment he came on board we cast off our moorings, ran up the jib and foresail, and slid rapidly away from the shore. The wind was moderately fresh from the northward, so we started under mainsail, foresail, and jib, but with the topmast lowered, as, being in very light trim, I did not think it advisable to run any risks by crowding sail upon the barkie.

We found, as I had expected, that on an even keel she was crank, though not to the extent I had anticipated ; but as she began to heel over her overhanging topside supported her ; so that, as the breeze freshened (which it did gradually), the more she lay down to it the stiffer she became.

As our confidence in her stability and sail-carrying powers thus became established, we grew
anxious to try her paces, and forthwith got her
topmast on end, the rigging set up, and put the
square-headed gaff-topsail upon her.   This was a
very large sail for the size of the vessel, though,
like the mainsail, it was not particularly high in
the *hoist;* but both sails were very much peaked,
the gaff-topsail so much so that the yard was
almost straight up and down.

With the setting of our big topsail an immediate
and very marked improvement in speed became
manifest.   Before this we had been darting along
at a very respectable speed, passing some smart-
looking schooners as though they had been at
anchor; but now the little craft fairly rushed
through the water, making it hiss and smoke
under her sharp bows, and leaving a long wake of
bubbles behind her.   She heeled over still more of
course, but it was with a steady kind of resistance
to the force of the wind which did finally away
with any lurking fears we might have had that we
were over-sparred or over-sailed.

We hove our patent log, and found that we were

spinning along a good eight knots through the water ; and indeed we came up with, and passed with ease, several vessels which were being towed down the river.   Bob and I were enchanted, and Mr. Wood scarcely less so ; and when, shortly after luncheon, he stepped into the boat which he had hailed to put him on shore at Gravesend, he said, " I am sure the little craft will come with credit out of the ordeal through which you are going to put her, whatever it may be ; so, gentle-men, I hope you will favour me on your return with a full account of your and her adventures."

We took leave of him with a hearty shake of the hand, and a faithful promise that we would do so (a promise which I intend to fulfil by sending him a handsomely-bound copy of this " log " as soon as printed) ; let draw the foresheet, and resumed our course down the river.

We met with no adventure worthy of record on our passage down, unless I except the amusement we derived from the chagrin of the crew of a French steamer bound to Havre, who, to their amazement, found that the little English yacht, by cutting off corners, skimming across shoals, and similar manœuvres, was slowly drawing ahead of them ; and though, after passing Sheerness, she gradually crept ahead of us at first, yet as the wind freshened, and we continued to "carry on" until the water was over our deck on the lee side half way up to the companion, we actually overtook and passed her, until, to escape an ignominious defeat, she set her own sails, and so drew away from us.

By eight o'clock that night we were off the North Foreland, bowling along at a slashing pace, with our mainsail boomed out to starboard, and our spinnaker set on the port side, jib and foresail stowed.

It was a glorious summer evening, and there was every prospect of its being a fine night ; the aneroid evinced, if anything, a tendency to rise, and there was a good slice of the moon left, though she would be rather late in rising, so we determined to keep going all night.

By ten o'clock we were flying through the Downs ; and very ticklish work it was to thread in and out between the ships at anchor there and those beating up, without experiencing a jibe, but by dint of a sharp look-out we did it.

By midnight we were off Dover, and here we took in the spinnaker, jibbed the boom over to port, and set our jib and foresail. Bob wanted the spinnaker set again on the starboard side; but I would not agree to this, as, though we had both been on deck hitherto, he insisted on taking the middle watch alone, while I went below for a four hours' sleep, and I did not think it prudent to leave him alone with so large and unmanageable a sail.

I wanted to take in the gaff-topsail also, but Bob would not hear of such a thing. He insisted that she was under easy and manageable canvas, and that there was nothing like making a passage while we had the opportunity. In this sentiment I fully agreed with him; but still I thought it better to err on the safe side, at least for the present, until we had become better acquainted with the capabilities of the craft. But Bob was obdurate, and at last I had to give in and rest content with the assurance that he would give me timely warning if it should become necessary to shorten sail.

When I came on deck at four o'clock I found

we were just off Dungeness, and in the midst of an outward-bound fleet of ships of all sizes and almost all nations. The wind appeared to have freshened somewhat during Bob's watch ; but the morning was beautifully clear and fine ; and, as our spars seemed to bear with the utmost ease the sail we were carrying, I thought we might venture to try the effect of a little extra " muslin."

Accordingly, before relieving Bob at the tiller, I roused out our spinnaker again ; and as we had hauled up a couple of points for Beechy Head just as I came on deck, I got it to the bowsprit end and set it, with its sheet led aft to the main-boom end, in place of the jib, which, with the foresail, I stowed. Bob then went below and turned in, first giving me strict injunctions to call him at " seven bells," that he might turn out and prepare breakfast, for it now appeared that he intended to unite the functions of chief mate and cook and steward, on the voyage we had just started upon so auspiciously.

The substitution of the spinnaker for the jib and foresail made a very great difference in our rate of sailing. When I first came on deck I noticed some distance astern a splendid clipper-ship, bowling along with every stitch of canvas set that would draw, up to skysails and royal studding-sails. By the time I had got my spinnaker set she was abreast of us, about half a mile outside and consequently to leeward. But *now* she was unable to draw away from us an inch, so great was our speed through the smooth water; and when Bob came on deck at "seven bells," she still lay as nearly as possible in the same position with regard to us as when he went below.

" Phew !" whistled he, as his eye fell on her, " so the big chap has found his match, has he, in a craft the size of his own long-boat. My eyes ! Harry, but this here *is* a little flyer, and no mistake. Why the post-office people 'll be wanting us to carry their mails for 'em if so be as they gets to hear on us, eh, lad ?"

Closing this remark with a chuckle of intense satisfaction and a leer at our big neighbour, Bob dived below again ; and shortly afterwards a frizzling sound from forward, and an odour strongly suggestive of bacon and eggs, which was wafted upwards from the companion, informed me that he had entered upon the duties of the less dignified but equally important part of his combined self-appointment.

We made a hearty breakfast off the aforesaid bacon and eggs, with *soft tack* laid in the day before, and washed all down with some most excellent coffee, in the concoction of which beverage Bob was an adept, and then, as soon as he had washed up, and put matters to rights in his pantry, and made arrangements for dinner, I went below and turned in until noon.

When I went upon deck again, I found that the breeze had softened down very considerably, and we were slipping along barely five knots through the water. Our big neighbour, the ship, could do nothing with us in such light airs, and he was now a good six miles astern.

During the afternoon, the wind dropped still more, and by eight o'clock in the evening we had little more than steerage way.

The water was absolutely without a ripple; our sails flapped, the main-boom swung inboard with every heave of the little craft over the long, gentle undulations of the ground-swell; and the different vessels in sight were heading to all points of the compass.

It was, to all appearance, stark calm ; yet there must have have been a light though imperceptible air, for on looking over the bows there was a smooth unbroken ripple stretching away on each side, showing that we were moving through the water still, though very gently ; and the fact that the little craft answered her helm was additional testimony to the same effect.

During the night a little air came out from off the land, and we mended our pace somewhat ; but it was not until the following noon that we got fairly abreast of St. Catherine's Point.

About eight o'clock the same evening, the wind still being light, we were abreast of the Needles ; about a couple of miles to the westward of them, and apparently steering pretty nearly the same course as ourselves, we saw a cutter yacht about our own size.

By midnight we were abreast of Durlstone Head, and had gained so much upon the other cutter that we could make out that she had a large and apparently a very merry party on board.

Hearty peals of laughter came frequently across the water towards us from her, and occasionally a song, generally with a good rattling chorus.

We continued to creep up to her, and at length got abreast of and so near her that, with the advantage of a good run, an active man might have leaped from one vessel to the other.

As we ranged up alongside, a most aristocratic-looking man stepped to leeward, and, grasping lightly with one hand the aftermost shroud, while with the other he slightly lifted his straw hat in salute, he inquired:

"What cutter is that?"

"The *Water Lily*, Royal —— Yacht Club," replied I. "What cutter is that?"

"The *Emerald*, Royal Victoria," answered our new acquaintance. "You have a singularly fast vessel under you," continued he; "I believe I may say she is the first that ever passed me in such weather as this. I have hitherto thought that, in light winds, the *Emerald* has not her match afloat; yet you are stealing through my lee as if we were at anchor. I presume, by the course you are steering, that you are, like ourselves, bound to Weymouth. If so, I should like to step on board you when we arrive, if you will allow me. I am curious to see a little more of the craft that is able to slip away from us as you are doing, in our own weather. I am Lord ——," he explained, thinking, I suppose, that we should like to know who it was who thus invited himself on board a perfect stranger.

I shouted back (for we were by this time some distance ahead of the *Emerald*) that I should be happy to see his lordship on board whenever he pleased to come ; and then the conversation ceased, the distance between the two vessels having become too great to permit of its being continued with comfort.

It was now Bob's watch below ; but the night was so very close that he had brought his bed on deck, and was preparing to "turn in" on the weather side of the companion for his four hours' sleep. As he arranged the bedding to his satisfaction, he cast his eyes frequently astern to the *Emerald*, whose sails gleamed ghostly in the feeble light of the moon, which, in her third quarter, was just rising.

"By George, Harry," exclaimed he, "if they *Emeralds* bain't shifting topsails, I'm a miserable sinner! Aye, there goes his 'ballooner' aloft. His lordship don't like the looks of our tail, seemin'ly; but I doubt whether, in this light breeze, his big topsail will enable him to catch us. My eyes! how we *did* slip through his lee, sure enough! Tell ye what, Harry lad; that topsail of our'n is a good un—a *rare* good un for a reach, and in a moderate breeze; but we ought to have a 'ballooner' for running off the wind in light weather—a whacking big un, with a 'jack' as long as the bowsprit, and a yard as long as the lower-mast. I'm beginning to think we are under-sparred and under-sailed."

I could scarcely agree with Bob in this. It is true that in fine weather we could carry considerably more canvas than we had; but I had a thought for the heavy weather also, and I knew that as soon as it came on to blow we should find our present sails quite as large as we could manage. Nevertheless, I made up my mind that we *would* have a balloon-topsail, as the voyage would be a long one, and it was possible that we might have spells of light winds for days together, when such a sail could be carried to the utmost advantage.

Notwithstanding the change of topsails, we still continued to creep away from the *Emerald*, and when we let go our anchor in Weymouth Roads, about six o'clock the next morning, she was still a good three miles outside of us; the wind had, in the meantime, fallen away so light, that it was not until after we had breakfasted that she drifted slowly in and brought up close to us.

Shortly afterwards, Lord —— came on board, accompanied by two or three friends; and his astonishment was great when he found that we only mustered two hands, all told. He noticed the absence of a boat from our decks, and inquired whether we had lost ours, and was still more astonished when we informed him that it was taken to pieces and stowed snugly away below.

This led to a request that he might be allowed to see it; and gradually it all came out that we were bound on nothing less than a voyage to the Pacific.

He was by no means inquisitive; his questions were merely such as one yachtsman would naturally put to another. But we knew beforehand that it would be difficult to conceal the fact that we were not merely cruising for pleasure; so we had come to the conclusion that it would be best to put a bold face upon the matter, and state at once that we were going a long trip; and Bob had proposed that, in the event of any questions being asked, we should give out that we were going to seek for some traces of my father.

To this I willingly agreed, as I really meant, if possible, to endeavour to find some clue to his fate; though I could not help acknowledging to myself that, if we *did* make any discoveries, it would be by the merest accident.

Lord —— seemed to be singularly struck with the model of the *Water Lily;* the only fault he found with her being the deficiency of head-room below. This fault, however, was inseparable from her peculiar shape, for, as I have already stated, she had a very shallow body, and a flat floor; and although she drew seven feet of water aft, her depth below her platform was entirely taken up with the ballast and water-tank, leaving only a height of four feet between the top of the platform and the under side of the beams; she was, in short, an exceedingly small craft for her tonnage.

We went ashore in his lordship's boat at his invitation; and as I casually mentioned that I meant on the morrow to put our "boat" together and give her a trial, he very kindly offered to accompany us in the *Emerald*.

My sister was, of course, delighted to see us both, and equally delighted to hear how thoroughly satisfied we were with our little vessel. It was evident that she had not quite conquered her apprehensions on the score of our long voyage in so small a craft; but our eulogiums upon the *Water Lily's* many good qualities were so enthusiastic, and the confidence we expressed in her sea-going powers so thorough, that Ada soon came to regard the voyage as in no degree more perilous than it would have been if undertaken in a vessel of four or five hundred tons.

We did not think it necessary to point out to her that we should probably be exposed to many perils besides those of the sea; and so the dear girl became satisfied, and learned to contemplate our speedy departure with comparative equanimity.

The next morning we made arrangements with a boatman for the hire of his punt during the short time that we intended to remain in Weymouth, as we wished our tubular boat to come into use only when we had no other to fall back upon.

Having struck our bargain, Bob and I jumped into the hired punt, and rowed off to the *Water Lily*, which lay at anchor in the roadstead.

It was necessary to pass close to the *Emerald* to reach our own craft, and as we pulled under her stern, Lord —— hailed us to know whether we still intended to make our trial trip, and, if so, how long it would be ere we should be ready.

I replied that I hoped to be ready in about an hour, whereupon his lordship jumped into his boat . to pay a visit to the post-office, saying he would be back in time to go out with us.

As soon as we got on board the *Water Lily*, we got our tubes on deck, screwed the different sections together, and launched them overboard. The framework connecting the two tubes together, and supporting the stage or deck, was next fixed ; then the deck itself, which was in three pieces, and so contrived that, when properly put together and laid in its place, a single bolt secured the whole immovably. Our centre-board and rudder were soon in their places, and nothing remained but to step the mast and bowsprit, set up the rigging, bend sails, and be off.

These latter operations took but a very short time, as every device had been adopted which would facilitate the boat's equipment ; and, having timed ourselves, we found that our boat was ready and under weigh *within* an hour of the time at which we had first begun to work at her. We considered this very smart work, but we hoped to shorten the time considerably after a little practice.

We took a few turns in the bay, whilst the *Emerald* was getting under weigh, and tried a few manœuvres with perfect success. There was only one thing about which we had any doubt, and that was whether she would *stay* or no. In the smooth water close to the shore (the wind was strong, from the south-west that day) she tacked beautifully, head-reaching a long way in stays ; and later on in the day we found that in this respect rough water made very little difference to her, owing to the peculiar shape of her tubes.

It was blowing a strong breeze from the south-west, as I have already said, and we took down a reef in our mainsail, whilst the *Emerald* started under trysail and jib, keeping her mainsail stowed so as not to run away from us.

We intended to run out round the *Shambles* light-ship and back; but as soon as I got clear of the bay, and from under the lee of the *Nothe*, I hauled sharp upon a wind to test the stability of my craft. To my astonishment, she did not appear to feel the effect of the wind at all, except as it tended to urge her through the water. She skimmed along very fast, but stood quite upright. Under these circumstances we, of course, shook our reef out and bore up for a run away to leeward.

The *Emerald* could do nothing with us at this game, much to the chagrin of her noble owner; so she was obliged to in trysail and set her mainsail, whilst we hove to and waited for her. But even after her mainsail was set we had the advantage of her.

She was a regular racer—long, lean, and deep in the water; whilst we floated entirely upon the surface, the tubes being exactly half submerged, as we noticed when we first started. The consequence was that we skimmed along like a feather, whilst the *Emerald* had to displace many tons of water with every foot of progress which she made.

We passed through the opening in the magnificent breakwater which shelters the roadstead at Portland, and soon afterwards began to feel the heave of the Channel. Our tube-boat rushed along over the crests of the waves with a very easy and steady motion, but the *Emerald* started rolling; and as we drew farther off the land, and got more into the influence of the rough water, this rolling motion became so violent that her boom had to be topped up pretty high to prevent it from dipping and dragging in the water every time she rolled to leeward.

Bob sat watching her attentively for some time, and at length—

" Aren't this here *Emerald* the little eight-tonner as took so many prizes last year in the regattas ?" said he.

I replied that she was.

"Well," said he, "we beat her all to nothing in a calm, or next door to it, last night in the *Lily*, and I'm thinking we could run her under water in a breeze like this here, with such a jump of a sea as we shall get when we rounds to on our road back. What's your idee, my lad?"

"I think we could," replied I. "She is so long and narrow that she must be a regular wet one close hauled, as I expect we shall see shortly. If I remember rightly, all her prizes were won in light winds or smooth water; and though I do not believe we could do anything with her in a staggering whole-sail breeze in *smooth* water, I fancy we could give a good account of her in a Channel match. But you must bear in mind, Bob, that the *Lily* is the larger craft of the two."

"That I deny," retorted Bob. "Heavier we may be as to tonnage, accordin' to the way tonnage is measured; but she's got double our power. I'll bet my 'lowance of grog for the next month to come that she's got good seven ton or more of lead stowed away under her cabin floor; whilst we've got two, besides the trifle in our keel; and *power*, as you know well, Harry, is what tells in a breeze. Take us all round, and, in spite of our difference of tonnage, I reckon we're pretty much of a size, and consequently a very fair match, so far as that goes. I should like to be alongside of her in the *Lily* in such a breeze and such water as this."

By this time we were close to the light-ship, still leading, and in another minute we shot under her stern and hauled up on the port tack. We now felt the full strength of the breeze, and I was somewhat alarmed to find how fresh it was blowing. But we were as stiff as a house, and could have carried half as much sail again, had there been more to set. We lowered our centre-board just before hauling up, and now we found ourselves tearing along in a manner which perfectly astounded me.

Our long, slender, pointed tubes appeared to offer no resistance whatever to our passage through the water. The motion was delightfully easy and gentle, the tubes piercing the body of each wave, as it rolled towards us, without the slightest shock, and lifting us gently and easily over the cap of it just as it seemed upon the point of coming in upon our deck. There was not an atom of spray ; we were as dry going to windward as when running free.

With the *Emerald* it was very different. Her huge mainsail was almost too much for her now that she was hauled close upon a wind; and as we looked astern, we could see her taking plunge after plunge, and sending her sharp bows clear through the seas at every dive, until her jib and foresail were wet half way up to their heads, whilst her lee-rail was completely buried in the boiling surge.

Now that we were close hauled, the *Emerald* walked up to us, though by no means so rapidly as might have been expected. There was no comparison between the powers of the two craft, yet, though we certainly dropped to leeward a little more than she did, it was *only* a little; and the difference in our speeds was very trifling, considering the great difference in size between the cutter and ourselves.

About a quarter of an hour after we rounded the light-ship, the *Emerald* passed us close to windward. She presented a most beautiful sight, at least to a nautical eye, as she swept by. She was heeling over to such an extent that the water was up over her deck, on the lee side, nearly to the skylights and companion ; and her immense sails were driving her so irresistibly through the short, jumping seas, that she had no time to rise to each as she met it. Her bowsprit plunged deeply into the advancing wave, her sharp bows cleft it asunder, and then, as they rose through it, amidst a blinding shower of spray, the water shipped forward, rushed foaming aft and to leeward like a swollen mountain torrent, until it mingled with the water which flooded her decks to lee-ward.

As soon as she was past us, her crew hauled down a couple of reefs in her mainsail, and set a smaller jib. This, of course, relieved her very materially, and, if anything, rather increased than diminished her speed, as she kept sailing round and round us with ease, until we were well over towards Weymouth Roads once more, and it had become perfectly evident that we needed no look-ing after.

As soon as he was quite satisfied of this, Lord —— made the best of his way to the anchorage, and brought up, having had such a dusting as ought to have satisfied him for some time to come.

As for Bob and myself, we were as pleased with our novel boat as it was possible to be. She proved to be a perfect success in every way; and when we took the tubes to pieces to stow them away, we found that, so accurately had the joints been made, that not a drop of water had penetrated to the interior of either.

One alteration, however, we resolved to make, and that was in the size of the sails. The boat was stiff enough to carry much larger sails than we had provided for her; and as we did not know but that a time *might* come when speed would be a matter of the most vital importance to us, we determined to furnish her with sails as large as it was prudent to carry.

We also decided to alter her rig somewhat, by substituting what is known among the initiated as a "sliding gunter" for a gaff-mainsail. This gives you a mainsail and jib-headed topsail in one, whilst it does away with the gaff altogether, whereby you obtain a much flatter standing sail; indeed, when this sail is properly cut (and it is not a difficult sail to shape), there is nothing to beat it in this respect.

Accordingly, we despatched an order to Lapthorn that night for the new suit of sails, and also for a balloon-topsail for the *Water Lily*, the dimensions of which satisfied even Bob, greedy as he was for canvas.

Meantime, the remainder of our stores were ordered, received, and shipped, and ten days after our arrival in Weymouth Roads we had everything on board which we could think of as necessary or likely to be in any degree useful to us on our voyage.

But when all was shipped, we found we had made a mistake somewhere in our calculations, and not only had rather more room than we expected, but our little craft still floated rather higher than her regular load-line. We therefore took in half a ton more lead ballast, which brought her down to within an inch of her proper trim, and with that we determined to rest satisfied.

CHAPTER V.

On the evening of Wednesday, August 8th, 18—, having wished all our friends good-bye, and pressed my last kiss upon the lips of my sobbing sister, I ran hastily down the flight of stone steps before my aunt's front door, crossed the road, and walked briskly down the Esplanade until I overtook Bob, who had gone on before me ; we then proceeded together to the New Quay end, found the man of whom we had hired our punt, paid him his money, and got him to row us on board the *Water Lily*.

We had arranged to start at daybreak on the following morning ; but as we pulled off to the cutter we remarked that there was a nice little breeze blowing from the westward, and as the evening was beautifully fine and clear, with the promise of a brilliant starlight when the night should have fully set in, the idea occurred to us both that we might just as well be getting on down Channel at once, as be lying at anchor all night.

Accordingly, as soon as we got on board, we loosed and set our canvas, hove up our anchor, and in half an hour afterwards were slipping through the opening in the Portland Breakwater.

In little more than half an hour after that we were clear of the dreaded Bill, when, noticing that a small drain of flood-tide was still making, we hauled our wind on the port tack, and stood in to-wards Bridport for an hour; then tacked again, and stood out towards mid-Channel, so as to obtain the full benefit of the ebb-tide, which by this time had begun to make.

By "six bells," or seven o'clock, on the following morning we were abreast the Start, about six miles distant. We stood on until eight o'clock, when we tacked again towards the land, having now a flood-tide against us, and had breakfast.

By noon we were in Plymouth Sound, when we made a short leg to the southward until we could weather Rame Head ; then went about once more, stretched across Whitesand Bay until the ebb-tide began to make again, and then again hove about and stood to the southward and westward, on the starboard tack.

At six o'clock that evening we passed the Lizard lighthouse, distant two and a half miles, and here we *took our departure.*

For the benefit of those who may be ignorant of the meaning of this expression, I may as well explain that the commander of a vessel *takes his departure* from the last *well-known* point of land he expects to see before launching into mid-ocean, by noting, as accurately as he possibly can, its compass-bearing and distance from his ship at a particular hour.

With these data he is enabled to lay down upon his chart the exact position of his ship at that hour, and from this spot the *ship's reckoning* commences. The courses she steers, and the number of *knots* or nautical miles (sixty of which are equal to sixty-nine and a half English miles) she sails every hour, together with certain other items of information, such as the direction of the wind, the direction and speed of the currents, if any, which she passes through, and the state of the weather, the *lee-way* the ship makes, etc., etc., are all entered in the log-book ; and at noon every day, by means of certain simple calculations, the ship's position is ascertained from these particulars.

The entering of all these particulars in the log-book is termed *keeping the dead reckoning*, and the working out of the calculations just referred to is called *working up the day's work*.

This, however, only gives the ship's position *approximately*, because it is difficult to judge *accurately* of the amount of lee-way which a ship makes, and it is not at all times easy to detect the presence of currents, both of which produce a certain amount of deviation from the apparent course of the ship.

To correct, therefore, all errors of this kind, which are otherwise impossible to detect when the ship is out of sight of land, various observations of the sun, moon, or stars are taken, whereby the *exact* latitude or longitude (or sometimes both together) of the ship at the moment of observation is ascertained.

This short lesson in navigation over, we will now rejoin the *Water Lily*, which we left at six p.m. off the Lizard, on the starboard tack.

It was my "eight hours out" that night, and when I took the tiller at eight o'clock we were dashing along a good honest eight knots, under whole canvas and a jib-headed gaff-topsail. The night was as fine as the previous one, but with a little more wind, and we were just beginning to get within the influence of the Atlantic swell. There was no sea on, but the long, majestic, heaving swell was sweeping with stately motion towards the Channel, rising like low hills on either side of us as our little barkie sank between them, and gleaming coldly, like polished steel, where the moon's rays fell upon their crests. But the little *Lily* sprang gaily onward upon her course, mounting the watery ridges and gliding down into the liquid valleys with the ease and grace of a seabird, and without throwing so much as a drop of water upon her deck.

The serenity and beauty of the night, the brilliancy of the stars which studded the deep purple vault above me, and the gentle murmur of the wind through the cutter's rigging, combined to produce a sensation of solemnity almost amounting to melancholy within me, and my thoughts flew back to the beloved sister I had so recently parted with, wondering whether she was at that moment thinking of me, or whether we should ever meet again, and, if so, how long hence and under what circumstances; and so on, and so on, until I was recalled to myself by a sprinkling of spray upon my cheek, whereupon I awoke, in the first place, to the fact that the breeze had so far freshened that the *Lily* was flying through the water with her lee gunwale pretty well under; and, in the second, to the knowledge that I had outstayed my watch a good half hour.

I lost no time in calling Bob, and as soon as he came upon deck we got our gaff-topsail down and our topmast housed.

I then went below and turned in; but I had time, before leaving the deck, to notice that we went through the water quite as fast (if not a trifle faster), now that our lee gunwale was just awash, as we did when it was buried a couple of planks up the deck in water.

When Bob called me at the expiration of his watch, I found, on going on deck, that the wind had continued to freshen all through the four hours I had been below, and it was now blowing quite a strong breeze. It had gradually hauled round to about north-west, too, which brought it well upon our starboard quarter, and we were flying along at a tremendous pace, with all our sheets eased well off.

But although by this change we were running *off* the wind, and consequently did not feel its full force, I decided to take down a single reef in the mainsail, and shift the jib; for there was a windy look in the sky that seemed to promise a very strong blow shortly. I did not wish to disturb Bob when perhaps about half way through his four hours' sleep, so I got him to assist me in making my preparations before he left the deck. And the promise was amply fulfilled as the sun rose higher in the sky, the wind freshening rapidly, but hauling still farther round from the northward as it did so.

By the time that Bob came on deck again, at seven bells, to prepare breakfast, I had my hands full. The sea was fast getting up, and I began to tremble for my spars and gear. The glass had fallen rather suddenly, and altogether there seemed to be every prospect of a regular summer gale.

Bob was of the same opinion as myself in this respect, so we decided to get everything snug and in readiness for the blow before thinking of breakfast.

This was rather a ticklish job, for it was now blowing far too strong to round-to and shorten sail, and it required something more than fresh-water seamanship to get our big mainsail in without getting into trouble. But Bob seemed perfectly at home. He set the weather-topping-lift up hand-taut, and took a turn with the lee one; then dropped the peak of the mainsail until the end of the gaff was pressing against the lee-lift; triced the tack right up to the throat; then let run the throat-halliards, and hauled down the throat of the sail by the tack tripping-line; whilst I rounded in upon the main-sheet. Then, by lowering away the peak, and carefully gathering in the canvas as it came down, we got our big sail snugly down without any trouble. This we carefully stowed and covered up with its coat.

Next, Bob got the jib in, close-reefed the bowsprit, and set the smallest or *storm* jib, with its sheet eased well off. I hauled in the weather fore-sheet until it was just in the wake of the mast, and our little barkie was then left to take care of herself whilst we got the trysail bent and set.

This done, we filled away again upon our course, with reduced speed, it is true, but very comfortably indeed.

It was well we took these precautions when we did, for by noon that day it had hardened down into a regular summer gale, with a really formidable sea for so small a craft. Still, we continued to run away very nearly dead before it, and that too without deviating from our proper course.

I managed, with the utmost difficulty, in consequence of the violent motion of the boat, to get an observation at noon, by which I found that we had run, since six o'clock on the previous evening, a distance of no less than one hundred and sixty-four miles. This placed us at about the entrance to the Bay of Biscay, which we were thus running into in a gale of wind. Still, I did not experience the slightest degree of alarm : our little craft was behaving beautifully—*angelically*, Bob termed it, and really it almost merited the expression. As she fell away into the trough of the sea, our low sails would become almost becalmed under the lee of the following wave ; but as she lifted with it, the wind would again fill them out, and she would dart away again just in time to escape the mishap of being *pooped* by its breaking and hissing crest.

At four p.m. I again succeeded in obtaining an observation, this time for the longitude. On working it up, we proved to be rather to leeward of our proper track ; so we hauled up a point or so, and at six o'clock decided to try what she was like when hove-to.

Watching an opportunity, we brought her to the wind on the starboard tack, first stowing our foresail, and found, to our great delight, that she rode like a gull. Beyond an occasional shower of spray, she shipped not a drop of water, although the gale was still increasing, and the sea rising rapidly.

We took a reef in our trysail, afterwards hoisting the gaff as high as it would go, so as to avoid, as much as possible, being becalmed in the trough of the sea, and then we were snug for the night.

Bob was a veteran seaman, and I had been in many a heavy blow before this—in gales, in fact, to which this was a mere nothing, comparatively speaking; yet neither of us could help feeling impressed—and for myself I may say somewhat awe-stricken—at the sublimity of the scene as the evening closed in. Hitherto, our experiences of gales of wind had come to us with a good, wholesome ship under our feet; but now we found ourselves face to face with one in a mere *boat*, little more than a toy craft. The sea, though nothing like as high as I had frequently seen it before, now wore a more formidable aspect than I could ever have believed possible. The hackneyed expression of "running mountains high" seemed strictly applicable; and I fairly own to having experienced, for, I believe, the first time in my life, a qualm or two of *fear* on that night.

The liquid hills, their foaming ridges as high as the top of our lower-mast, swept down upon us with an impetuous fury which seemed irresistible;

and the effect was further heightened, as darkness closed around us, by the phosphorescent glare and gleam of their breaking crests. But the *Lily* rose lightly and buoyantly to each as it rushed down upon her, surmounting its crest in a blinding shower of spray, and then settling easily into the trough between it and the next one.

The roaring of the gale, too, and the angry hiss of the storm-lashed waters, contributed their quota to the feeling of awe with which we looked abroad from our pigmy ark.

But confidence returned after a while, as we watched the ease with which the little craft over-rode the seas; and when I at length turned into my hammock, it was with a sense of security I could not have believed possible a couple of hours before.

We hoisted a carefully-trimmed and brilliant lamp well up on our fore-stay as soon as night closed in, for we were in the track of the outward-bound ships going to the southward, and should one of these gentlemen come booming down upon us before the gale during the night, it would be rather difficult to avoid him.

It was well that we took this precaution, for no less than five passed us in Bob's watch, and three more in mine, one of them coming near enough to hail; but what he said it was impossible for me to hear, the howling of the wind and the hissing of the water so close to me utterly drowning the words.

I conjectured, however, that it was some inquiry as to whether we wanted assistance of any kind, and on the strength of this supposition I roared back at the top of my voice:

" All right; very comfortable."

A figure in the mizzen rigging waved his hand, and the noble craft (she looked like an Australian liner, and was carrying topmast and lower stun-sails) swept onward, and was soon afterwards swallowed up in the darkness and mist.

The falling in with so tiny a craft so far at sea, and in a gale of wind, and the announcement that she was "all right and very comfortable," must have been rather a novel experience for them, I imagine.

About noon next day the gale broke, and by four o'clock the wind had gone down sufficiently to justify us in making sail and filling away upon our course once more. This we did by setting our reefed mainsail, foresail, and No. 2 jib. The wind had continued to haul round too, and was now pretty steady at about north-east. This rapidly smoothed the water down, so that we had a comparatively quiet night; and the wind continuing to drop, we shook out our reefs next morning at eight bells, and got the big jib and small gaff-topsail upon her.

The evening but one following we got a glimpse of Cape Finisterre about six o'clock, and this enabled us to corroborate our position. From this point we shaped a course for Madeira, and after a splendid run of seven days from the Lizard and eight from Weymouth we arrived at Funchal at half-past five o'clock on the Wednesday evening following that on which I took leave of my dear sister.

As Bob was busy below getting tea, and I was stowing the canvas, a steamer came in with a flag flying, which, on taking a look at it through the glass, I recognised as the distinguishing flag of the Cape mail-boats, so I left everything just as it was, dashed down below, and penned a few hasty lines home, giving a brief outline of our adventures so far, and taking care not to lay too much stress upon the gale, whilst I was equally careful to do full justice to the *Water Lily's* sea-going qualities, that my sister's apprehensions might be as much allayed as possible.

As soon as I had finished and sealed the epistle I joined Bob upon deck to assist him in putting our novel boat together, which done, we pulled on board the mail-boat, where we were very kindly received; and I gave my letter into the hands of the captain, who promised (and faithfully redeemed his promise too) to post it on his arrival home.

I afterwards found that he reported us also, so that the *Water Lily* duly appeared in the "shipping" columns of the various papers, and my yachting friends thus got an inkling of our success thus far.

I shall not attempt any description of Madeira, or indeed of any other of the well-known spots at which we touched. The places have been so often and so fully described in the many books of travel which have been written, that any further description, or at all events such description as I could give, is quite superfluous. It will suffice for me merely to say that Bob and I spent three days stretching our somewhat cramped limbs in this most lovely island, and discussing which route we should take to the Pacific.

We had often discussed this question before; but it was with a feeling of indifference which precluded our arriving at any definite and absolute decision upon the matter. It was now, however, time that this point was settled, as it would affect our course soon after leaving the island, or, at all events, when we came to the Cape de Verdes.

The eastern route would be much longer than the western; but I felt disposed to adopt it, in the belief that we should be favoured with much better weather. I entertained a very wholesome dread of the "Horn"—the notorious "Cape of Storms." Bob, on the other hand, was all for the western route.

" I'm willin' to allow," observed he, "that a trip round the Horn ain't like a day's cruise in the Solent—all pleasuring; but I've knowed ships to come round under r'yal stunsails, and that more than once. The place is bad enough ; but, like many another thing, not so black as it's painted. It's got a bad name, and that, we know, sticks to a place or to a body through thick and thin. I've been round five times, twice outward-bound and three times homeward, and we always had plenty of wind ; but only once did I round it in a reg'lar gale, and then, had the *Lily* been there, I'll lay my grog for the rest of the v'yage she'd have made better weather of it than the old barkie I was aboard of. It's risky, I know ; but so's the whole trip for that matter, though, so far, by what I've seen of the little craft, I'd as lieve be aboard *her* in a gale of wind as I would be in ere a ship that ever was launched. She's cramped for room, and when you've said that you've said all as any man can say ag'in her. Besides, see how 'twill shorten the v'yage. Once round the Horn and you're there, as you may say, or next door to it. And then, there's ' Magellan ;' if, when we get down about there, things don't look promising for a trip round outside of everything, ram her through the Straits. I've been through 'em once, and an ugly enough passage it was too, blowing a whole gale; but there's *thousands* of places where the *Lily* would lie as snug as if she was in dock, but where a large ship dursen't venture for her life."

I yielded, as I generally did in such matters, to Bob's judgment; and it was settled that the *Water Lily* should brave Cape Horn with all its perils. On the fourth day of our stay at Funchal we filled up our water-tank, made a few additions to our stores (among others, a small stock of the famous wine produced by the island); and towards evening stood out to sea again, with our main-boom well garnished with bunches of bananas and nets of various kinds of fruits; the wind at the time being light, from about east-south-east, with a fine settled look about the weather. This lasted us for four days, and ran us fairly into the "trades," and on the third day following, just as the sun was dipping beneath the horizon, we sighted St. Antonio, the westernmost of the Cape Verde Islands.

The "trades" were blowing very moderately as it happened, and the weather was as fine as heart could wish, with a nearly full moon into the bargain, so we were able to carry not only a jib-headed topsail, but also our spinnaker at the bow-sprit end ; and under this canvas the little beauty made uncommonly short miles of it, tripping along like a rustic belle going to her first ball. We fell in with several homeward-bound ships, all of whom we requested to report us on their arrival as "all well." So fine a run had we from the Cape de Verdes, that on the morning of the fifth day after sighting them we ran into the "dol-drums" or region of calms and light variable airs which prevail about the line.

Here our light duck did us valuable service, for though the wind soon fell so light that it became imperceptible to us, and not a ripple disturbed the glassy surface of the water, by getting our enor-mous balloon gaff-topsail aloft we managed to catch enough wind from *somewhere* to fan us along at the rate of nearly three knots. True, the breeze was very variable, our boom being sometimes on one side and sometimes on the other, sometimes square out (at least as far as the little air of wind had power to project it), and sometimes hauled close in as the flaws headed us, and broke us off two or three points one side or the other of our course.

But, in spite of the baffling airs, such good progress did we make, that by two o'clock that afternoon we were gliding slowly through a fleet of
about forty sail of vessels which were so completely becalmed that they were heading in all
directions, utterly without steerage-way.

We reported ourselves to such as we passed
within hail of, and finally, about four o'clock,
ranged up alongside of and boarded a beautiful
little barque of about three hundred and fifty tons,
whose monkey-poop we saw full of passengers
(some of whom were ladies), regarding us with
the utmost curiosity as we approached. She
turned out to be from Natal, bound to London;
and her captain (a perfect gentleman both in
appearance and manner) not only promised to
report us, but gave us a hearty welcome on board,
and so cordial an invitation to dinner that there
was no resisting it.

Our story, or at least as much of it as we chose
to tell (which was simply that we were taking the
cruise partly as an adventure, and partly with the
object of seeking intelligence of my father), was of
course soon drawn out of us; and, naturally

enough, it excited the liveliest astonishment in the minds of our hearers, and soon got all over the ship. We excited some curiosity on board the other ships too, for no less than four captains lowered their boats and pulled alongside to learn where the pigmy cutter had sprung from.

The little craft was regarded with the greatest curiosity and admiration, especially by the ladies (who are of course good judges of the model of a vessel), some of them declaring that they would be *delighted* (with strong emphasis) to make a voyage in such a little *darling* of a yacht.

We mustered quite a strong party at the dinner-table, what with the regular party, the four visiting captains (who were also pressed to stay), and our two selves, and a very merry one withal. *We* contributed to the dessert from our stock on the main-boom; and they only who have enjoyed it can say what a luxury is fresh fruit on the line, especially when one has been a long time on board a ship.

The skipper produced unlimited champagne (of which, for a wonder, he still had a very fair stock) in honour of the occasion, and "a prosperous voyage, and success to the *Water Lily*," was drunk over and over again that evening. We kept it up until nearly midnight, the poop being converted into a ball-room by merely hanging a few lamps in the mizzen-rigging ; the orchestra consisting of one of the seamen, who played the concertina better than I ever heard it played before or since.

The weather being as I have described it, with out any signs of a change, such a departure from the ordinary routine of the ship was permissible, and I have no doubt everybody on board was glad enough of an occurrence which gave such an excuse for breaking in upon the monotony of the voyage.

Tedious enough they must have found it, for it appeared that they had already been becalmed five days, and had not altered their position as many miles ; and there seemed every prospect of their being becalmed five days more, for the glass was as steady as if the mercury had been solid.

At last we visitors made signs of moving. The captains of the other vessels ordered their crews into their boats, and I was just about going over the side on my way to our small cabin to write a hasty line to Ada (our kind host having promised to post my letter for me immediately on his arrival), when a seaman stepped up to me, and with the usual nautical scrape of the foot and a respectful " Beg pardon, sir," intimated a desire to speak to me.

" There's a strange yarn going the rounds of this here craft's fo'c'sle," said he, "about your bein' on a sort of v'yage of discovery a'ter your father, sir."

I said, " Certainly ; it was perfectly true."

" Well, sir," said he, "maybe I might be able to help you in your search. It needs no prophet to tell that you are Captain Collingwood's son, when a man gets a fair squint at your figure-head, axing your pardon, sir, for my boldness ; and if you'll just give me your word that nothing I may say shall tell agin me, I'll tell you all I knows about it, and gladly too ; for I sailed with your father, sir, and a kinder skipper or a better seaman never trod a deck than he was, as I've had good reason to know."

"*Was?*" exclaimed I, with a sudden sinking of heart.

"And is still, for aught I know, sir; at least I hope so; there's no reason why he mayn't be still alive," replied the man, fully understanding all the meaning of my exclamation.

"Thank God for that," replied I fervently. "But why is this strange pledge required? Surely, fellow, you will not have the temerity to tell *me*—his son—that he has been the victim of any foul play? If so——"

"Not on *my* part, sir, I'll take my Bible oath," said he. "What I did I was *forced* to do to save my own life. Gladly would I have helped the skipper if I could; but what can one man do agin a whole ship's crew."

"*Much*, if he have the will," replied I. "I will give no pledge whatever, beyond this. Tell me your story, and if I find you were powerless to prevent the evil which I begin to suspect has befallen my poor father, you have nothing to fear; but if I find that you have in any way aided——"

"Never, sir. If I could have had my will the

skipper would not be where, I suppose, he is now ;
but you shall hear all I have to say, and then
judge for yourself whether I could prevent anything that happened or no."

CHAPTER VI.

THE FATE OF THE "AMAZON."

THE man who, in this unexpected manner, brought me intelligence of my father, belonged to the crew of one of the visiting captains' boats, and a word or two of explanation was sufficient to procure the delay in the boat's departure necessary to permit the fellow to tell his story.

In order to be a little more alone, Bob (who was, in a few words, made acquainted with the facts of the case), the seaman, and I went down over the side to the *Water Lily's* deck, when, as soon as we had comfortably bestowed ourselves, the man thus began :

"You must know, gentlemen, to commence with, that I was shipped, among others, on board the *Amazon* at Canton. Dysentery was awful bad among the crews just at that time, and no less than seven was ashore from our old barkie bad, when she left. Two chaps run as soon as she got in, and couldn't be found agin ; so there was nine berths in the fo'c'sle to be filled when she was ready to sail. As I was sayin', I was one of the new hands shipped. Englishmen was scarce somehow just then, and the skipper had to take what he could get. Consequence was, he shipped three Portuguese, a Spaniard, a Greek, two Frenchmen, and a Yankee, besides myself. The third mate was ashore bad, and the second mate had died, so the Yankee (who seemed a smartish sort of chap) was made second mate, and one of the old fo'c'sle men was put into the third mate's berth. When we got aboard, we found the hatches on, and all ready for a start, and that same a'ternoon we unmoored, and away we went.

"We was the first ship as went away with any of the new teas, and the skipper was awful anxious for a quick run home. We carried on night and day ; but the weather was light with us, and we didn't get along half as such a smart ship ought to ha'

done, for she was a reg'lar flyer, as perhaps you
gentlemen both knows.

"Well, we hadn't been out above a week when,
whether 'twas worryin' at the light winds, or what
'twas I can't say, but the poor skipper was laid on
his beam-ends with fever, and it took the chief
mate all his time to prevent his jumping overboard.   However, it didn't seem to matter so
much, so far as the ship was consarned, for the
Yankee second mate turned out to be a first rate
navigator, and he in a way took charge of the craft.

"Well, gentlemen, how it all came about, I
can't say, for I never noticed anything wrong.
True, some of the chaps talked a bit queer to me
at times ; but I thought 'twas all a bit of a flam ;
but, howsomever, one fine night my Yankee
gentleman and the new hands takes the ship.   At
eight bells in the first watch, the watch below was
called ; and as soon as they came on deck three on
'em goes straight over and jines the mutineers
without a word ; so it was clear as 'twas all
planned afore among 'em.   That left only three
whites out of the plot—the Lascars had all been
bribed or frightened into jining in with t'others—

and, out of us three, two was lying on deck, lashed hands and heels together when I come up through the fore scuttle.

"The minute my foot touched the deck, I was tripped up and secured before I was fairly awake, and stowed alongside of the two other chaps. Then my noble Yankee, he steps up and stands in front of us three, and he says, says he, 'Now you chaps, you see how it is; we've got the ship and we means to keep her; and we've made up our minds to do a little bit of pirating; make our fortunes; and then cut the sea and live like gentlemen for the rest of our days ashore. If you've a mind to jine us, well and good; if not, there's a plank sticking over the bows, and I'll be obliged to trouble you to take a short walk on it for the benefit of your constitooshuns. You've got five minutes allowed to make up your minds.'

"When the time was up, one of the chaps was unlashed, and the Yankee asks him what he intends to do.

"'I'll walk that ——— plank, if I must,' says he; 'but I hope I'm too honest to turn my hand to your —— pirating,' says he.

"'All right,' says the Yankee; 'just as you please; there's no compulsion; only if you're so confounded honest,' says he, 'you'll have to leave this here ship,' says he, 'for we can't afford the room to stow away sich a bulky article as honesty. That's your road, and a pleasant passage to ye,' says he, pointin' to the plank.

"Poor Bill—I can see him now, it seems to me —he stood for about half a minute looking far away into the moonlit sky, thinking of his friends, maybe, if he had any; and then, without a word, he steps to the rail, puts his hands upon it, jumps up on to the top of the bulwarks, and next minute there was a splash alongside, and he was gone.

"T'other chap was then cast adrift, and *he* was asked the same question.

"'I've sailed with Bill,' says he, 'for nigh on six years, and never knew a truer-hearted ship-mate, or a better seaman,' says he; 'and since it *must* be, here goes,' says he 'to take our last cruise in company.'

"And he too jumps upon the rail just as Bill did, and, without waitin' a second, launches himself overboard a'ter him.

"It was now my turn. I'd been thinking matters over in my mind whilst all this was going on ; and I'll confess I found it hard to make up my mind to die. 'Whilst there's life there's hope,' thinks I ; 'and it can but come to a launch over the side at last, if the worst comes to the worst ;' so when they asked me what I intended to do, says I, 'Tell me, first of all, what's become of the skipper ?' says I.

"'He's below in his bunk,' says the Yankee, 'and the mate with him, and there they're welcome to stay so long as they don't interfere with us,' says he, 'and I'll take good care they don't,' says he. 'But what's that to do with you ?'

"'Well,' says I, 'I likes the skipper ; he's been a good friend to me, and I couldn't be content to see harm come to him. If you'll promise to shove him ashore all safe,' says I, 'I don't mind taking a hand in your little game.'

"'Very sensible indeed,' says the Yankee ; 'you've a darned sight better notions in your head than they two stupid cusses as has just gone over the side with nothin' to ballast 'em but their —honesty,' says he ; 'and as for the skipper—

make your mind easy. We've no grudge agin him ; all we wants is the ship ; and now we've got her, we means to put the skipper and the mate both ashore somewheres where they can be snug and comfortable like together, but where there'll be no chance of our hearin' anything more from 'em for the rest of their lives.'

"And that's the way it was all settled," continued the man. "I made up my mind I'd never do no pirating if I could help it ; and I thought maybe if I stuck to the craft, I might be able to help the skipper a bit somehow, and if ever I got a chance, why, I'd make a clean run for it, and I reckoned I should find a way to do that the first port we touched at.

"Well, as soon as matters was arranged, the Yankee takes the command, and makes the Greek chief mate ; the watches was divided, the course altered, and away we goes to the east'ard, on the starboard tack, with a taut bowline and everything set as would draw, from the skysails down. One hand is told off from each watch to keep a look-out in the cabin ; and the steward has his orders to do everything he could for the poor skipper.

He had a hard time of it, poor man, for when he was getting better, and the truth couldn't any longer be kept from him, the mate told him what had happened, and the news took him so completely aback that he got as bad as ever again, and the wonder is that he didn't slip his cables altogether. However, he managed to hold on to 'em, and at last the fever left him ; but he was that weak he hadn't strength to turn over in his berth without help.

" All this time we were going to the east'ard, or about east-south-east, with everything set that the spars would bear. At last, about a month or maybe five weeks after the mutiny—I didn't keep much account of the time—we fetches up, all standing, one dark night, upon a coral reef, before we knowed where we was. There warn't much sea on, and we happened to touch where there was nearly water enough to float us ; so we bumped and thumped gradually right over the reef into deep water—at least about ten fathoms—on t'other side. The well was sounded, and we found five feet of water in the hold ; so, as there was land of some sort close aboard of us, the Yankee rams her straight on to it to save her from sinking under us.

" When daylight broke, we found ourselves on the sandy beach of a small island, with reefs all round us; but a space of about a quarter to half a mile of clear water everywhere between the reefs and the island.

" The cargo was roused out, and the ship examined, as well as it could be done, to learn the extent of the damage, for the Yankee talked about careening her to repair her bottom; but we soon found that the job was too much for us. So we stayed on the island about a week, fitting out the launch and the pinnace; and when all was ready, and everything stowed in the boats that it was thought we should want, we made sail to the nor'ard and east'ard; not, however, until the rest of the boats had been destroyed, and the skipper and mate made all snug and comfortable like in a tent ashore."

" Then you were inhuman enough," exclaimed I, "to leave my poor father, sick as he was, on a desert island ?"

" He was better off there than he would ha'

been with us," replied the man. "The island was a first-rate spot, with cocoa-nuts and bananas, and lots of other fruits, no end ; plenty of fresh water, and the bulk of the ship's stores to draw from. It was a *lovely* spot ; lots of shade, pure air, and pretty nigh everything a man could want, what with the stores, and the fruit, and so on. He *must* have died, had we taken him away in the boats, for the sun beat down upon us *awful*, and the heat was reflected back from the surface of the water to that extent we was nearly roasted.

"Well, we'd been to sea nigh on to three weeks, and was getting pretty short of water, though we touched at a couple of islands and filled up again, on our way, when one evening— there wasn't a breath of air blowing—we sighted a sail to the nor'ard of us. She was becalmed, like ourselves.

"The Yankee takes a good long look at her, or at least at her to'gallants'ls, which was all we could see, and then tells us he'd made up his mind to have a slap at the chap during the night. We carefully took her bearings, dowsed our canvas, and pulled leisurely towards her. At last, when we thought we were beginning to near her, we muffled our oars, and then paddled on again, both boats within oar's length of each other.

"We pulled for about an hour, and then waited for some sign of her whereabouts—for we reckoned we must be close aboard of her—but it was that dark you couldn't see the length of your nose. After waiting a goodish spell—none of us speaking a word for fear of giving an alarm—we hears eight bells struck, somewhere away upon our port quarter.

"We had passed her, so we pulled very quietly round and just paddled in the direction we thought she was lying. In about five minutes the Yankee says, 'I see her,' says he; and we stopped paddling. The pinnace was hanging on astern of us, so's we shouldn't lose one another in the dark; and she was hauled up, the men in her told what to do, and the ship pointed out to them; and then we pulled away very quietly again.

"By this time we could just make out a dim something towering up in the darkness, which we knew to be her sails. In another minute our boat was alongside on her starboard quarter, and the pinnace on her larboard quarter ; we shinned up her low sides, and before the watch on deck could rub their eyelids open, we had her.

" She turned out to be a little Yankee brig, with a cargo of sandalwood, and was bound to Canton.

" Some of her crew joined us, the rest—the poor skipper and the first mate among 'em—was hove overboard, and the sharks had a good meal. She mounted four sixes, and had a well-stocked arm-chest, so that, with the arms we brought with us from the old *Amazon*, we was pretty well off. We mustered a good strong crew too—twenty-nine altogether, counting the Lascars—so, as the brig was a beautiful model, and, we soon found, sailed like a witch, our skipper decided to set up for a pirate at once.

" Well, gentlemen, it kept stark calm for two whole days after we'd took the brig, and Johnson —that was the Yankee's name, Edward Johnson —he kept us all busy during that time disguising the craft, by painting the hull and spars afresh, and such like ; and the carpenter he was sent over the starn on a stage to fix a plank over the name, on which he'd carved a lot of flourishes and such like, and the word *Albatross*, which was what Johnson had re-christened her, and by the time we'd finished, her own builder wouldn't have knowed her.

"After everything was finished to his satisfaction, he calls us all aft, and tells us that he'd been thinking matters over, and he'd decided to take the ship to Hong-Kong, and get rid of the sandalwood there, and get a lot of things that was wanted to complete our outfit, and make us fit for a good long cruise.

"Accordin'ly as soon as the breeze sprang up, away we goes, never falling in with anything as Johnson thought it worth his while to meddle with all the way.

"We had a pretty quick run, for the brig sailed quite wonderful; and all the while I was turning over in my mind how to get away. I intended to take the first chance as offered, as soon as we got in; but Johnson was a 'cute chap, none of us was let out of the ship any more'n he could help, and then only they as he knowed he could trust.

"At last the cargo was out and the ballast in, the brig cleared for the South Pacific, and everything ready for sailing next morning, and I'd had no chance to get away, and I was beginning to think things were looking queer with me. But I didn't give up all hope, for I knowed a chance *might* offer at the last minute, if I was but ready to take it.

"Some time during the night I woke up and went on deck for a minute or two, and found it as black as pitch. There wasn't a soul moving in the ship. I don't know where the anchor watch was, stowed away asleep somewheres, likely. Anyhow, I thought to myself that now was my chance, so, without waiting another minute, I climbs over the bows, and lets myself quietly down into the water by the cable. As soon as I was adrift, I lets the tide take me, for I was afraid of makin' so much as a splash whilst I was near the ship. I drifted astern for about five minutes, and then struck out. I hadn't taken no bearings, and didn't know where the shore was ; but I saw a few lights, and I shaped a course for them.

"But after I'd swam about a matter of twenty

minutes I found I was farther away from 'em than I was when I started; and then the thought flashed into my mind that the tide must be on the ebb, and that I was going out to sea. I was so took aback that I went under. But I didn't feel like giving up without I was obliged; so I struggled to the top of the water again, and then turned over on my back to think matters over a bit. But I didn't find much encouragement that way; and I was beginning to think it was all up with me—'specially as I was getting pretty tired—when I heard a sound some distance away, like a coil of rope hove down on deck.

"I started to swim in the direction of the sound, and after perhaps about five minutes I makes out something away on my port bow. I gives a shout as loud as I could, and that sends me under again; so I soon found that game wouldn't answer.

"However I stretched out as hard as I could, and got alongside; but there warn't nothing to take hold of, and she slips past me. I was too done up to sing out again; but I starts to swim after her, when I strikes my head against something, and it turns out to be a boat towing astern. I got hold of the gunnel, and managed somehow to get aboard, and then down I goes into the bottom of her, too exhausted to do anything.

"I dropped off to sleep pretty soon, and was only woke up when the chaps came to hoist their boat in.

"The craft turned out to be a coasting junk, bound to Shanghai, as I managed to make out, but not another syllable could I understand of their lingo or they of mine 'twould seem.

"Blest if the very next night we wasn't run down by something or other—I never knowed what 'twas, for they hadn't the good manners to stop and pick us up.

"The mainmast of the junk was knocked out of her in the smash, and I managed to get hold of it and lash myself to it, just in the eyes of the rigging. The yard happened to be undermost, and so I had a pretty good berth.

"I floated about on that —— spar for four days and nights without a bit or drop of anything, and then my senses broke adrift, and I knew nothing more of what happened to me for some time

" When I came to myself I found I was on board a Dutch ship, homeward bound. It turned out that they passed close to my spar, and seein' me lashed to it they picked me up.

" At least so I made it out; but I knew no Dutch, and there was only one chap aboard that thought he knowed English ; but Lord bless ye, gentlemen, *I* couldn't make top nor tail of what he said. I manged to make out hows'ever that I'd had a narrow squeak of it, and that's about all.

" By the time I was able to get about on deck again, we was well out in the Indian Ocean, and everything seemed going on all right ; but, as it turned out, it was all *wrong*, for early one morning we makes land ahead, the wind bein' light and dead on shore.

" The skipper hauled sharp up on the port tack to try and claw off ; but a current had got hold of us, and away we sagged to leeward, do what we would, and at last we had to anchor.

" By-and-by the breeze freshened ; but we was in a very ugly berth, and the skipper didn't like to make a move.

"However, we didn't have a chance to settle the matter for ourselves, for just about sunset the old barkie struck adrift, and, before we could get the canvas on her, she was in among the rocks and bilged.

"We all got ashore, there bein' no great matter of a sea running, and, to make a long story short, was made prisoners by the natives. What become of the rest of the hands I never knowed—they may be there yet for all I can say. An old chap picked me out, and made a sort of servant of me, and, on the whole, I had pretty easy times of it. I got to find out, at last, that I was somewhere on the island of Madagascar.

"I stayed here nigh on two years, I reckon; but at last I got a chance to steal a canoe and slip off to a small craft that was becalmed in the offing. She was luckier than the Dutchman, as we got a breeze off the land about an hour after I boarded her.

"She was bound to the Cape, and there I left her, shipping the very same day in the craft I now belong to, and sailing for home the same a'ternoon."

"Well," said I, as soon as the man had finished, "if your story is true—and I see no reason to doubt it—*you* at least are blameless as far as the wrong done to my father is concerned. The only question now is, whereabouts is the island on which he was left?"

"Ah, sir," replied he, "that's more'n I can tell. I *did* hear Johnson mention the latitude and longitude of it once; but I'm blest if I can remember 'em now."

I was determined, however, to get *some* clue if possible, however faint it might be; and I took him into our little cabin, and spread a chart of the Pacific on the table. Then I got him to recall, as nearly as he could, the courses and distances steered by the *Amazon* until the time of her wreck.

We managed to trace her as far as the north-western extremity of New Guinea, the man happening to remember hearing Johnson point out some land in sight as the Cape of Good Hope.

This must manifestly have been the headland of that name on the north-west coast of New

Guinea; but from this point he became be-
wildered. He remembered passing a great many
islands after sighting this headland, however, and
was of opinion that the average courses steered
were about south-east, and he thought it was
nearly a month afterwards when the ship was lost.

This placed the scene of the wreck on one of
the islands in the large group in which we expected to find our treasure-island.

I questioned the fellow until I found I had
extracted really every particle of information it
was in his power to give, and then, after reward-
ing him for his information, I let him go.

As soon as he was gone, I wrote a hasty note
to my sister, cautiously conveying to her the
intelligence that we had obtained a faint trace of
the *Amazon's* fate ; a trace which, I added, we
intended to follow up as far as we could, and
having sealed and addressed my missive, I
hurried up over the barque's side, and placed it
in her captain's hands, and then took leave of him
with a hearty shake of the hand and many good
wishes on his part that we might have a safe and
pleasant voyage.

It was time we were off, for a gentle breeze was springing up, and all parties were anxious to avail themselves of it to the utmost extent.

As soon as we had once more got all our light canvas spread, Bob, instead of turning in as he had a right to do, it being his watch below, came and sat down beside me, and we began to discuss the strange story to which we had so lately listened.

" It has enabled me definitely to make up my mind upon one point, which I will now confess has troubled me not a little," said I, "and that is your proposal to go round the 'Horn,' Bob. Ever since we settled upon that route, I have been thinking of the great risks we must run by adopting such a course, and I really think that, but for this, I should have hauled sharp up upon the port tack as soon as we fell in with the southeast trades. *Now*, however, I feel so anxious about my father, and his condition, that I would incur double the amount of risk, if need were, in order to reach the Pacific as soon as possible, and, Bob, we must find *him* before we give a thought to the treasure.

"Right you are," exclaimed Bob heartily; "and there's my hand upon it, Harry, my lad. The treasure can wait; but it may be of the greatest consequence to the skipper to be found as soon as possible. He may be ill, or tormented by a parcel of cannibal savages, or a thousand things may be happening to him to make it important for him to have a couple of trustworthy hands like ourselves added to his crew as soon as may be. So shove the huzzey's nose as straight for the Cape as she'll look, and let's get that part of the job over as soon as we can. And as to the *danger* of the expl'ite, we'll weather it somehow. The little beauty has showed us already what she can do, and with a couple of prime seamen—which I take it no man will deny *we* are—to handle her, take my word for it, she'll carry us round as safe as e'er a craft that floats."

"There's another thing I've been thinking of within the last hour," continued I. "We talked of going into Buenos Ayres when we first made up our minds to take the route round the Horn; but even that short detention I should now like to avoid if possible. Want of water is really the only cause which would *compel* us to call there, though I confess I should like to write a line to Ada from thence, to let her know we had safely reached so far——"

"As to the first," interrupted Bob, "I feel no consarn whatever. We are pretty certain to fall in with heavy rains afore we get very far south ; and if the wind happens to be light we can easily spread one of the sails so as to catch the water, and one good heavy thunder-shower would fill our tank for us, and as to letters, why, we shall perhaps have such another chance as this here that we've just had, and that disposes of the second difficulty. If we *don't* get any rain before, there's a splendid harbour on the southermost side of the Gulf of St. Matias, hereaway on our starboard bow, somewheres about two or three days' sail to the south'ard of Buenos Ayres, and we can fill up our water there. I've been into the place once, and a fine snug anchorage it is."

This was a great relief to me, for in my present feverish state of excitement it seemed to me that any stoppage, unless absolutely unavoidable, would be more than I could endure.

By this time it was Bob's watch on deck ; but I felt that it would be utterly impossible to sleep if I turned in, so I insisted that he should go below instead, and, after some argument, he consented.

In about ten minutes more, certain sounds arising through the companion told me that my friend was too thorough a seaman to be kept awake by excitement, and I found myself alone and at liberty to indulge in the new hopes which had so lately been awakened within my breast.

CHAPTER VII.

THE SEA-SERPENT.

THE breeze, though it continued light and rather baffling at times, still held when the sun rose next morning; and on looking astern, I found that the homeward-bound ships had all disappeared; and of the outward-bound craft, our light heels had enabled us to get so far ahead that the topsails of the nearest were already dipping. Of course light winds and smooth water made exactly our kind of weather; and the enormous spread of our lighter sails caused the little craft to slip through the water in quite an extraordinary manner, whenever we could show them. There was just enough wind to barely ruffle the surface of the gently swelling ocean, yet our patent log told

us we were going rather over six knots, mainly
through the persuasive influence of our spinnaker
and gigantic balloon topsail.

At noon our observations showed that we
were nearly a degree south of the line; and
I began to be sanguine that the breeze we
now had would run us into the trades. In this,
however, I was disappointed; for about sundown
the wind fell so light that we barely had steerage
way. All night long it continued the same, and
the greater part of next day; and for about
sixteen hours I considered that we did not
advance more than a knot per hour.

Towards the close of that afternoon, however,
when I came on deck to take the first dog-
watch, Bob directed my attention to the appearance of the sky in the south-eastern quarter,
announcing it as his opinion that there was a
look of the trades about it. And so it proved,
for the breeze gradually freshened, and drew
more round from the eastward, and by eight
bells we were doing our nine knots, with a nice
fresh breeze.

This was doubtless the first of the south-east trade-wind; for by midnight it had so far freshened that, for the sake of our spars, it became necessary to take in our spinnaker and balloon topsail, and to substitute for them the working jib and our jib-headed topsail. Even this would have been deemed perilous sail for so tiny a craft by most persons; but we were by this time thoroughly acquainted with the *Lily* and knew that she would carry with ease all the canvas that her spars would bear.

Nothing particular occurred for the next two days. The wind held, and continued to blow with a force which was, for us, a good, staggering breeze, but without much sea; and we kept flying to the southward at a pace which left even my impatience no reason for complaint.

On the second day after getting the breeze, we passed the Brazilian mail-boat near enough to show our number in the yacht-list, and to ask him, by signal, to report us "all well."

The next morning it was my watch on deck until noon. Bob had cleared away the breakfast, carefully washing up everything, and stowing an hour.

I was enjoying the fresh beauty of the morning, and the exultant feeling excited by our rapid motion; and picturing to my imagination the delight with which my father would welcome the appearance of our snowy canvas—when we should heave in sight, when my visions were dispersed by a loud, cracking sound like the report of a rifle, from some distance away on our weather-bow. I looked in that direction, and caught a momentary glimpse of some distant object whirling in the air, and immediately afterwards the sound was repeated.

I stood up to get a better view over the low ridges of the sea, and at the same instant caught sight of what looked like a jet of steam rising out of the ocean.

"There she blows!" exclaimed I, involuntarily aloud.

Again up whirled the object I had before observed; again it descended, and again came the rifle-like report.

I knew in an instant now what it was. An

unfortunate whale had fallen in with his in-
veterate enemy, a "thresher," and had been
forthwith attacked. I could plainly distinguish
the huge creature plunging along at a great
rate, and at an angle of about forty-five degrees with our course; so that he was standing
in such a direction as would take him across our
bows.

From the persistent manner in which he
remained at the surface, I came to the conclusion
that he had a second enemy to contend with in
the shape of a sword-fish. Indeed, the way in
which he began to plunge about, soon put the
matter almost beyond a doubt.

I was turning over in my mind whether I
should call Bob to see this sight, when the
whale, with a mighty effort, flung his huge
bulk completely out of the water, to a height
of, I should say, fifteen or twenty feet; and,
sure enough, hanging to him was a large
sword-fish, with his beak driven deep into the
muscles about the root of the persecuted animal's
tail.

I shouted to Bob to come on deck at once,

for we had neared each other so much by this time, that I had an excellent view of the combat.

And, moreover, it struck me that a slight deviation in the course of the combatants might bring them within extremely unpleasant proximity to the little *Lily*, and I thought it might be prudent to have Bob on deck.

He was up in an instant, not waiting to perform the almost superfluous ceremony of dressing, and there we both stood, so intensely absorbed in the interest of the exciting spectacle that the little craft was almost left to take care of herself.

The whale had got very nearly straight ahead of us by this time, and not more than half a mile distant.

Bob went forward, and stood leaning against the mast, to get a somewhat better view. Suddenly, the chase bore sharply up, and dashed away at tremendous speed in exactly the opposite direction to that which he had been pursuing before. Almost at the same instant Bob shrieked in a shrill unnatural tone of voice :

" Luff ! Harry—luff ! round with her for the Lord's sake ! Oh, my God !"

Down went the helm, and up flew the little *Lily* into the wind, and I was just stooping to let go the head-sheets (which led aft), when I caught a glimpse of Bob's face, white and drawn with horror, and his eyes—almost starting out of his head—staring fixedly at something apparently broad on our starboard bow.

I looked, naturally, in the same direction myself, and never to my dying day shall I forget the frightful, appalling object which met my gaze.

At a distance of not more than three cables' lengths from us, rushing through the water at a speed equal to that of a railway train, and lashing the water into foam with the rapid movement of his huge convolutions, a monstrous serpent appeared, darting towards the wretched persecuted whale.

His vast head and fully twenty feet of his body towered nearly erect above the water, and I believe I am not exaggerating, nay, that I am *within* the mark when I say that the remaining portion of his body, to the tail, was at *least six* times that length.

His head was shaped much like that of a python, and his enormous jaws, which he frequently opened, disclosed a formidable array of strong sharp fangs. His body was of a deep dead brown, broadly marked with irregular stripes and rings of pale stone-colour ; and he emitted a strong musky odour, which, even at our distance from him, was almost overpowering.

Once, when he was closest to us, he turned his head in our direction, and for one dread moment he paused, seeming to gather his folds together as though about to dart upon us, and the bitterness of a frightful death thrilled through me.

The next instant he sped on once more at still greater speed, and before another minute passed the whale was overtaken.

The ocean was, for a single instant, lashed into the semblance of a boiling caldron, we saw a rapid whirling movement of the creature's enormous coils, and then followed the deep bellowing cries of the tortured whale, and the crunching sound of its crushing bones.

During the minute or two which had passed since our helm was put down, the *Lily* had been lying to on the starboard tack; our head sheets still remaining fast on the starboard side.

The seizure of the whale awoke me, as from a horrible nightmare, to the fearful peril to which we still remained exposed; and I jammed the helm hard up, and wore the craft sharp round on her heel until dead before the wind, when I eased off the main sheet, and we hurried as fast as the wind would take us away from the spot.

As soon as we had got the *Water Lily* round, and were fairly running away from our dangerous neighbour, we both, with one accord, turned a look astern, to ascertain the condition of things in that quarter.

The serpent and the whale had both disappeared. Doubtless the former had sunk with his prey to those profound depths which form his usual habitat, there to enjoy his meal undisturbed.

"Well," at last exclaimed Bob, "I've been knocking about at sea now nigh on thirty year; and many's the strange sight these good-looking eyes of mine have looked upon in that time; but this here sarpent beats all. *I* never seed the likes of the thing afore, and I don't care if I never sees it agin. I've heern tell of such things bein' fallen in with, sartaintly; but I never could meet with a man as had act'ally seed the beast with his own eyes; and I put it all down as a yarn for the marines. But seein' is believin'; and we've had a good look at him, and no mistake. I'm quite satisfied; I don't want to see no more to make me a believer in sich things."

"No," replied I; "it was impossible to make any mistake, with such a view as we obtained of the creature; and I shall henceforward be far more ready than I have hitherto been to give credit to the accounts which are occasionally published of such appearances. I do not at all expect that *we* shall be believed when we make known our adventure, any more than others have been; but that will not alter the facts of the case.

The almost universal scepticism with which announcements of such creatures' appearances are treated is, after all, not very difficult to account for. They doubtless inhabit only the extreme depths of the ocean, and are probably endowed with the means of sustaining life whilst sunk for long periods—if not for an indefinite time—at those depths; it is easy, therefore (supposing such to be the case) to understand that it may be quite opposed to the creature's habits to appear at the surface *at all;* and that, when it does so, it will be—as, indeed, we have every reason to suppose—at very lengthened intervals; and then, probably, only in consequence of some unusually disturbing influence. The opportunities of seeing the reptile must necessarily, under such circumstances, be extremely few; and it is quite possible, or rather I should say, very likely, that many of its visits to the upper world have been entirely unwitnessed. In the present instance, for example, no eyes but ours were witnesses of the scene which so lately took place; and had we been but a dozen miles from the spot, it would have passed unnoticed even by us. And

my observation of mankind, Bob, has led me
to the conclusion that the race are extremely
sceptical as to the existence of everything but
what is *well* known."

"Very true, Harry, my lad," returned Bob;
"you reels it all off just like a book, and therein
you shows the advantages of larning. I knows
by my own feelin's how difficult 'tis to believe a
thing a man don't understand. But it seems to
me, 'to return to the practical'—as I've heard
the poor old skipper say—that we might as
well haul up on our course agin now; and I'll
go and look after the dinner; for I shall be
afraid to go to sleep agin for the next fortnight; that blamed old sarpent 'll ha'nt me
like a nightmare now, if I so much as shut my
eyes for five minutes."

The sheets were flattened in, and the little
craft's jaunty bowsprit once more pointed southward; whilst Bob dived below, and in a few
minutes more a thin wreath of smoke issuing
from the galley-funnel betrayed his whereabouts,
and his occupation.

Suddenly he reappeared at the companion, and with a serious countenance remarked :

" I say, Harry, lad, I s'pose there's no chance of that devil"—with a jerk of the thumb in the direction of our weather quarter—"getting a sniff of our dinner, and making sail in chase, is there ?"

I assured him that, in my belief, there was a strong probability that the serpent was, at that moment, perhaps *miles* deep in the ocean, banqueting royally on the dead whale; and, seeing the reasonableness of this supposition, he retired, satisfied.

Nothing further occurred that day to disturb us. We continued to bowl away to the south-ward; and as we kept our canvas a good rap full, the little barkie tripped along a good honest nine knots every hour. The weather was as fine as we could possibly wish, with every ap-pearance of being thoroughly settled; and there seemed to be a good promise of our making an exceptionally rapid passage.

It was my eight hours out that night; and when Bob relieved me at midnight the sky was

as clear as a bell; and, though there was no
moon, the stars were shining brilliantly, and
with that mellow lustre so peculiar to the
tropics.

Bob declared he was glad to be on deck again,
for he had been tormented, all his watch below,
by "that villanous sarpent;" visions of which
so disturbed his restless slumbers that it was
a real comfort to have the craft to look after, and
something to occupy his mind.

I anticipated no such disturbing influence
myself; for though I candidly confess I was
awfully frightened at the moment, the effect had
passed away almost with the disappearance of
the monster; and the cool freshness of the night
breeze had induced a feeling of drowsiness,
particularly welcome to a man about to retire to
his hammock.

In less than five minutes I was fast asleep.
When I awoke, which I did without being called,
I was surprised to find the sun streaming down
through the skylight; and still more so when
I observed that we seemed to have gone about
during the night. The *Water Lily* was now

certainly on the starboard tack ; whereas, when I turned in, we were on the port tack.

" It *can't* be a change of wind, here in the heart of the trades," thought I. " What can Bob be about ? and why has he allowed me to overrun my watch. Surely the old fellow was not *afraid* to come below, and turn in ? Hallo ! Bob ahoy ! what's wrong on deck ?" shouted I, springing out of my hammock.

Just as I did so, I heard the mainsail fluttering, as though the boat had luffed into the wind ; and at the same moment I caught sight, through the companion-way, of the vacant tiller swinging about.

" Gone forward to shift the jib," thought I ; and I jumped on deck to lend a hand.

Bob was nowhere to be seen.

" Good heavens !" exclaimed I, " what dreadful thing has happened ?"

I thought of the sea-serpent for one moment, but dismissed the idea the next, as being both too horrible and too unlikely.

The creature could hardly have approached without giving Bob the alarm, which I knew he would have instantly communicated to me.

At that moment my eyes fell upon the main-boom, and I missed the life-buoy which we kept suspended from it in readiness for any sudden emergency. Bob then had gone overboard, taking the life-buoy with him, and that too upon an impulse so sudden that there had been no time or opportunity to arouse me.

The *Lily* was indeed hove-to, as I had observed when I first awoke; but it was with *both* jib and fore-sheet to windward. The probability was then that, on Bob quitting the helm, she had flown up into the wind until her head sails were taken aback, when she would, of course, or *most probably*, pay off on the opposite tack, and remain hove-to. This must necessarily have happened *at least* four hours ago (it was now eight o'clock), because had Bob been on deck at eight bells, he would, of course, have called me. And during all this time the boat had been sailing away from him, not very rapidly it is true, being hove-to, but probably at a rate of at least three knots an hour. What might not

have happened to the poor fellow in that time ?
He was a splendid swimmer, I knew, having
acquired the art on our last voyage, and well
able to take care of himself in the water; and
there was very little sea on. Besides, I felt
pretty certain he had the life-buoy; and, with
its assistance, I knew he could keep himself
afloat in such weather until worn out with exhaustion from want of food. But there were
other perils than that of drowning; and, if
attacked by a shark, what chance had he ?

These thoughts flashed through my mind
whilst busily employed in taking the necessary
steps to return in search of him, for I had no idea
of continuing the voyage without making such a
search, indeed it would have been impossible.
And my chances of success were not so meagre
as might at first sight be supposed.

In the first place, knowing how difficult it
would be to see such an object as a life-buoy,
even with a man in it, at any great distance, from
so low an elevation as our deck, I had taken
the precaution to have each buoy fitted with a
contrivance for hoisting a signal.

This consisted of a small bundle of jointed rods, which could be put together like a fishing-rod, and on the topmost of these was a white flag two feet square. On the buoy itself was firmly lashed a step similar to the " bucket " (I believe it is called) in which a carriage-whip is placed when not in use by the driver. The rods, taken to pieces, were securely lashed in a compact bundle to the buoy, and the bucket was a fixture. Thus, if Bob had the life-buoy, he also had the means of indicating his whereabouts, and that, too, at a considerable distance. And I knew pretty nearly in what direction I ought to steer, in order to take the most effectual means of finding him.

Whilst hove-to, the *Lily's* course or drift was, on the whole, as nearly as possible at right angles to the direction of the wind. It only re-mained then to turn her round and keep the wind directly abeam, and I should be going back pretty nearly over the same ground I had been traversing since Bob went overboard.

Accordingly, I lost no time in getting the *Lily* round, when I once more hove her to, and went aloft to the cross-trees with my glass to see if the white flag were visible.

A long and anxious scrutiny followed, but without any discovery. I did not feel any very great disappointment at this, for I thought it very probable I was too far away to discover so small an object, even with the aid of my glass.

Once satisfied that it was nowhere to be seen, I quickly descended to the deck, trimmed the sheets flowing, and away the little craft bounded over the bright flashing sea.

I stood on for an hour exactly, when I once more hauled the fore-sheet to windward, and went aloft with my glass again.

My first look was ahead, first with the naked eye, and then with the glass; but not a speck could I discern to break the monotony of the blue-grey of the sea, except an occasional curling foam-crest. I next carefully swept the ocean from forward round to windward, thinking I might have run too far off the wind.

Once or twice I thought I detected a flickering of something white, but it instantly disappeared again; and I was obliged to believe it was only

the foam of a breaking wave. I was about to
descend once more to the deck, when it occurred
to me to take a glance to leeward.   I once more
levelled my glass, and swept it over the surface
of the sea ; but again I could see nothing.   I
reluctantly closed it, slung it over my shoulder,
and swung myself off the cross-trees to go down
by the mast-hoops, when my eye was arrested
for a moment by what I *knew* at once to be
the flag.

Almost as I caught sight of it, I lost it again ;
and as the craft was constantly falling off or
coming up again into the wind, I hardly knew
exactly in what point to look for it.   However, I regained by position upon the cross-trees,
levelling my glass, rather inconveniently, on the
fore side of the topmast, to clear the topsail,
and presently I caught it again.

Yes, there it was, sure enough, about three
miles dead to leeward ; and what was more, I
could not only see the flag, but also the buoy, and
Bob in it.   He seemed to be waving his arms
about in a most frantic manner, and making a
tremendous splashing, doubtless, I thought, with

the view of making his position more apparent, as, of course, he could see the cutter, and knew I must be looking for him.

I slipped down on deck, quick as lightning, triced up the main tack just high enough to enable me to see under the foot of the sail; and squared dead away before the wind.

Ten minutes afterwards I caught a glimpse of the flag right ahead, as the boat rose on a sea; and then I edged away, taking room to run up alongside him on the port tack with my head-sheets to windward. I could now see Bob away on the port bow, every time the *Lily* rose on the top of a wave; and he was still, to my great surprise, splashing away furiously; and now I caught the sound of his voice, shouting.

"Surely," thought I, "the poor fellow has not become insane through the dreadful strain to which his nerves have been subjected!"

A minute later the cause of his strange be-haviour became apparent.

A dark object of triangular shape appeared, moving in narrow circles round the spot where poor Bob was floating; disappearing at frequent intervals, and then the splashing became more frantically vigorous than ever. It was a shark that was thus blockading Bob, and the splashing was resorted to to frighten the creature from attacking him.

I carefully measured my distance, and exactly at the right moment jammed my helm hard down, hauling in the main sheet as I did so.

The *Lily* shot into the wind, just clearing the buoy by a hair's-breadth. I sprang to the rigging, stooped down, and seized Bob's extended hand with mine as he came alongside, and then, exerting all the strength I could command, I fairly jerked him out of the water upon deck, just as the shark had apparently made up his mind to be no longer denied.

With such impetuosity did he make his rush that his snout rose a good two feet fairly above our gunwale; and had not the impetus with which I jerked Bob out of the water been sufficient to fetch him clear inboard, the shark would have had him after all. As it was, we got a glance into his open jaws, and at his six rows of teeth, the remembrance of which makes me shudder to this day.

As the shark disappeared with a savage whisk of the tail, poor Bob turned to me; his lips quivered convulsively for a moment in an effort to speak, and then he fell to the deck in a dead faint.

Two or three buckets of water dashed in his face, and a glass of neat brandy, however, soon restored him, and it was almost pitiful to listen to the poor fellow's heartfelt and reiterated expressions of gratitude for his rescue.

" Ever since about half an hour after sunrise was that incarnate devil alongside of me," exclaimed he; "and hadn't it been for my seeing the cutter's sails, and knowin' as you was on the look-out for me, I *must* have give in. Human natur' couldn't hold out agin that sort of thing for long. And now, I feel that weak and done up, that a child might pitch me overboard agin, if he was so minded, I do believe."

The life-buoy came aboard again with Bob; so I unshipped the signal-staff and took it to pieces, made it up in a bundle once more, stopped it to the buoy, and slung the buoy itself in its old position on the boom.

The cutter was still hove-to, and I allowed her to remain so, whilst I went forward to see to the breakfast, Bob meanwhile changing his wet clothes for dry ones, and hanging the former in the rigging to dry.

I was still busy over the cookery, when Bob came into the forecastle, and observed :

"I say, Harry, there's that spiteful devil still alongside, and with a most onchristian longing to make a breakfast off of your old shipmate, I'll go bail! Couldn't we contrive somehow to put a stopper on his tormentin' purpensities ?"

"Aye, aye, Bob, old man!" replied I; "I think we may manage to do that without much difficulty. You get one of the air-guns out of the beckets, whilst I look after this coffee—it's just on the boil—and we'll try the virtues of cold lead upon his constitution, and the powers of the gun at the same time."

As soon as I could leave the coffee, I got a piece of pork out of our small harness cask, and lashed it to a piece of line, whilst Bob, under my directions, charged the gun. This done, the pork was hung just outside the taffrail, and full in the shark's view, but not in the water; and I lay down on deck with the gun ready for my gentleman, should he make a rush.

This, however, he seemed indisposed to do; eyeing the bait longingly, but keeping at a respectful distance. Gradually this distance shortened, however, and he finally ventured close under the boat's stern, and within about three feet of the pork.

I kept the gun levelled at him, aiming at his eye; and now, having him so close, and so directly under me, I thought there was little fear of the bullet being diverted from its proper direction by the water, so I fired.

The lead sped true; the blood spirted from the creature's eye, and with a tremendous spring he threw himself backward, only to roll over on his back with a convulsive writhe or two ere he floated motionless and dead.

"So much for bullyin' honest seamen when they has the misfortin' to walk overboard," observed Bob, eyeing the carcase with much complacency. " I shall feel more comfortable like, now I knows as *your* cruise is over for good and all."

" Walk overboard, Bob !" exclaimed I. " You surely do not mean to say you *walked* overboard ?"

" 'Twas little else, my lad. But I'll tell ye all about it whilst we're getting our breakfast stowed under hatches ; for I'll be bound you're longing to hear the rights of the story."

" That indeed I am, old fellow ; so come along below, and let us get the yarn and our breakfasts at once ; I am longing for both."

Having taken a look all round, to see that nothing was in sight, we went below and seated ourselves at the cabin-table, and Bob forthwith proceeded with his story.

CHAPTER VIII.

"You'll maybe remember," commenced Bob, "that when I came upon deck last night to take my watch, I mentioned that I was glad enough to be out of my hammock, and away from the tormentin' dreams I'd had of that —— sarpent !

"Well, and I was too—I felt better and calmer like the minute I set foot upon the deck ; and, as soon as you was gone below, I makes myself comfortable in the chair " (a low deck-chair in which we used frequently to sit whilst steering), "takes the tiller-rope in my hand, sets the little craft's course by a star, and starts thinking how pleased the skipper will be when he sees his son and his old mate turning up some fine morning at the anchorage which, I doubt not, lies just under his parlour window.

"I got thinking and thinking, until it seemed to me as I could see the 'old man' as plain as I can see you now, coming down between the trees, with his hand held out, and his face all smiling and joyful like, and I steps forward to give him a hearty shake of the fin, when all of a suddent he changes into that infarnal old sarpent, and at me he comes, with his eyes glaring, and his jaws wide open.

"You may take your oath, Harry, I warn't long in stays. Round I comes like a top, and away I scuds dead afore the wind; and he—the sarpent, I mean—arter me. It seemed to me as the faster I tried to run, the less headway I made; and presently he was close aboard of me.

"There was a great rock just ahead of me; and I makes a *tremenjous* jump to get behind it, when whack goes my head agin the main boom with that force it fairly stunned me, and afore I could recover myself I lost my balance, and overboard I goes.

"I felt myself going, and flung out my hands

to save myself naterally, and by that means I managed to get hold of the becket of the life-buoy, which in course broke adrift from the boom, and came overboard with me.

"Well, I didn't seem to know where I was or what I was doin' for a minute or two ; and then the cold water revived me. I slips my arm through the buoy, and takes a look round for the cutter.

"I must have run her pretty nigh dead off the wind in my sleep, for I could see her almost straight to leeward of me, still standin' on, but comin' slowly to the wind.

"She was a good quarter of a mile away from me, and I thinks as how I might still have a chance of fetching her agin, if she gets to luffing into the wind, and losing her way, so I strikes out a'ter her.

"But, Lord bless ye! Harry, you've no idea how the little hussy slips along, until you comes to be overboard, swimming in her wake.

"It seemed to me as though she'd *never* come to, and all the while she was walking away to the tune of a good seven knots.

"At last when I rose on the top of a sea, I sees

as she was in stays; and 'All right,' thinks I,
'Harry's come on deck and missed me, and he's
comin' back a'ter me.   But I soon saw as she'd
run into the wind, and hove herself to, and that
most likely you was still fast asleep in your
hammock.

"I next tried to cut her off by swimming in the
direction that she was heading, but after about
half an hour's hard tusslin' I knowed it was no
use; she fore-reached upon me as if I was at
anchor.   So I give the job up, and lay-to in the
buoy for a rest, for I'd put out all my strength in
chase, and was pretty nigh done up.

"I knowed you'd miss me some time in the
morning, and that you'd miss the buoy too, and
I felt sartain that you'd come back to look me up,
so I sets to work to get my signal-pole on end
and the flag flyin', all ready for daylight.

"I watched the little barkie fairly out of sight,
and then I began to feel lonesome like, and I'll
own that most oncomfortable thoughts came into
my head about the sea-sarpent; but, strange as
you may think it, I never give a thought to the
sharks.

" I thought as day were never going to break agin ; but at last I sees it light up a bit away to the east'ard, and it got grad'ally brighter and brighter ; and presently I sees the sun just showin' above the horizon.

" Then I felt a little bit more cheerful and satisfied like, for I knowed you'd soon be stirring, and I should have you back on the look-out for me.

" Of course I gave a good look all round as soon as there was light enough to see properly ; but there warn't so much as a gull in sight, and away to the nor'ard and east'ard where I knowed you was, the sun dazzled my eyes so's I couldn't see.

" Well, 'twas just as I'd caught a glimpse, as I thought, of the peak of the *Lily's* gaff-topsail, that I sees, about fifty fathom away, the fin of that —— shark scullin' quietly along. I kept pretty still, you may swear, hoping he'd pass me. But— not he. Down goes his helm, and he takes a sheer my way, and I thought it was all up with me.

" He ranged up alongside as quiet as you please, hows'ever, and just dodged round and round me, off and on, as if he didn't quite know what I was made of.

" I expect it was the flutterin' of the flag overhead as he didn't understand ; but, any way, he kept very quiet and peaceable for a good long spell, and I was beginnin' to hope he wouldn't have no truck with me. And, to cheer me up still more, I sees the little *Lily* coming back to look for her chief mate.

" If you'll believe me, Harry, I'm of opinion that devil saw you comin' as well as myself, and that he knowed he'd have to make up his mind pretty soon, or lose me altogether, for he began to swim round me now tolerable smart, and presently he makes a dive.

" I'd made up my mind what to do as soon as he took to that game ; and I starts splashing hands and legs all I knowed, and shouting too, like fury ; and presently he comes up again.

" Well, the chap kept me that busy, I hadn't a minute to spare ; and when you ranged up alongside I was that tired out I didn't know how to make another splash."

" So much for going to sleep in your watch on

deck, Master Bob," said I, as the mate brought his yarn to a conclusion.

"Aye! more shame to me that I should ever have done such a thing," replied he, greatly crest-fallen ; "but I lay the blame of the whole consarn, from beginnin' to end, on that —— sarpent, though no amount of sarpents will excuse a man fallin' asleep in his watch, more especially when he has charge of the deck."

"Well," said I, "you have been pretty well punished for your fault, old man, at all events. But 'all's well that ends well;' and I am heartily glad that you are so well out of the scrape. And now, I shall insist on your going to your hammock for the rest of the day, and I'll take care of the craft. In fact she will almost steer herself in this weather, so I shall manage very well indeed. Only don't have any more dreams which will cause you to jump overboard, please, for I really cannot afford to lose you."

The poor old fellow was so exhausted that, though he protested against the proposed arrangement, I could see he was glad enough to avail himself of it; and after a feeble attempt at remonstrance, he yielded to my persuasions, and turned in, and was quickly in a sound refreshing sleep.

Nothing further of importance occurred for several days to break the monotony of the voyage.

We continued to make good way to the southward, and ten days after crossing the line we lost the south-east trade winds, and ran into a light southerly breeze. As we still had a very fair quantity of water on board, and indulged in good hopes of getting rain enough, shortly, to fill our tank up, without the necessity of putting in anywhere, and as the chances were very great that, as we got farther to the southward, we should meet with westerly winds, I determined to stand to the southward and westward, close hauled, of course, on the port tack, so that *should* the wind come from the westward, as we expected, we should be in a good weatherly position; whilst, if we were disappointed in the matter of rain, we should have the land close aboard, and could run in and fill up.

The southerly wind lasted us a couple of days,

and then veered gradually round to about south-west.   As this broke us off considerably from our course, we hove the cutter about, and were then able to lie about south-and-by-east, a good rap full.

The wind now freshened considerably, and we had it stronger than at any time since leaving England, except in the gale in the Bay of Biscay, so that we were reduced to double-reefed main-sail, reefed foresail, and number three jib. Under this canvas the little *Lily* made very excellent weather of it, though the incessant showers of spray which she threw over herself necessitated the constant use of our macintoshes whilst on deck, and this we found extremely in-convenient, from their warmth.

However, as we had been wonderfully favoured in the matter of weather so far, we had no right to grumble if we were now treated to a few of the inconveniences of such a voyage as ours. Though still making very good way, we were not getting on so fast as we had been, our low canvas, and the heavy sea (for a craft of our size) which began to get up, not permitting us to do more than our seven knots.

Still, this was remarkably good work, and we ought to have been perfectly satisfied ; but the little barkie had stepped out at such a rattling pace all the earlier part of the voyage that we could not be contented with any reduction in speed.

This lasted for five days, and then, about one p.m., the wind suddenly dropped altogether, and left us tumbling helplessly about without even steerage-way. The sky had gradually become overcast, and the air suffocatingly close, and when I went below to look at the aneroid, I found it had gone back considerably.

This might mean only a thunderstorm, or it might mean something much worse, so we set to work to prepare for whatever might come. The mainsail was stowed and the cover put on, the foresail hauled down and unbent, and the trysail bent, reefed, and stowed, to be set or not as circumstances might require.

As it turned out it was only a thunderstorm, but it was a regular tropical one whilst it lasted.

The rain came down in *sheets*, without a breath of wind ; and we not only filled our tank, but also every available cask, can, and empty bottle we had on board, and as this was done long before the rain was over (though the thunderstorm soon passed off), Bob and I stripped, and enjoyed to our heart's content the unwonted luxury of a wash from head to foot in the most deliciously soft water, after which we roused out our dirty clothes. and had a regular good washing-day.

The rain lasted about three hours, and then cleared away as rapidly as it had come on, leaving the air beautifully fresh and pure, the sea beaten down until nothing but a long, lazy swell remained of the late breeze, and ourselves refreshed beyond description by our soap and water bath. The sun came out again, clear and strong, drying our washing in about half an hour, and to complete the good work, a nice, steady wind from the north-east sprang up, and sent us bowling merrily along upon our course once more, with all our flying kites aloft to woo the welcome breeze, the glass beginning to rise again immediately that the thunderstorm was over.

Two nights after this, the wind still holding favourable, though rather fresher, so that our spars had as much as they could do, notwithstanding our preventer backstays, to bear the strain of our enormous spinnaker and balloon gaff-topsail, and the little *Water Lily* flying along at —as our patent log told us—over thirteen knots, we dashed past a half-consumed hencoop, a few charred pieces of planking, and some half-burnt spars, all of which had the appearance of having been but a short time in the water.

The spars were those of a ship of about a thousand tons; and we came to the conclusion that it was one of those melancholy cases in which the good ship, after perhaps successfully battling with a hundred storms, is made to succumb at last to that terrible foe to seamen, a fire, ignited by the merest and apparently most trivial of accidents. But the reader will see, further on, that we had but too good reason to alter this opinion.

We passed this wreckage about the middle of the second dog-watch, while Bob and I were discussing the propriety of shortening sail somewhat for the night; but as the breeze seemed disposed to grow lighter rather than otherwise, we decided to let everything stand for the present.

When Bob called me at midnight, however, the wind had hauled so far round from the eastward that it became necessary to shift the spinnaker to the bowsprit-end; and this we accordingly did.

The wind had fallen much lighter while I was below, it continued to drop all my watch, and when I turned out next morning there was barely enough of it to fan us along at about three knots.

As the sun rose higher it died away altogether, and it was as much as we could do, through the day, to keep the cutter's head in the right direction. This would have been wearisome work in the tropics; but we had been out of them for some days, and were getting well to the southward, and the air began to feel quite fresh and chilly at night; so much so, indeed, that for the last night or two Bob and I had found our thick pilot jackets a very great comfort.

At last, by the time that tea was ready, the *Lily* was "boxing the compass," having lost steerage-way altogether ; so, as our big sails were no use, we took them in, and stowed them away, not knowing from whence or how strong the breeze might next come.

We took a good look all round at the weather, and then left the *Lily* to take care of herself, whilst we went below to our evening meal. This over, we both went on deck again to smoke our pipes, and have a chat until eight bells. It may be thought that two men situated as we were would soon exhaust all available topics of conversation ; but this was by no means the case.

Bob, though he had no education but that pertaining to his profession, was a profound thinker, and he often amused and sometimes startled me by the originality of his remarks.

He had knocked about the world a good deal, and had the knack of not only a quick observation, but also of being able to clearly and accurately recall what he had seen, and the impressions thereby produced upon himself.

He was expatiating, on this occasion, on the

charms of nature, of which he was an enthusiastic admirer, the subject having been suggested by the beauty of the sunset which we had both been watching, and I was thoroughly enjoying the rugged eloquence with which the scene had inspired him, when we were startled by a long, low, wailing cry which rang out upon the still air, apparently not half a dozen fathoms from us, making our blood curdle and our hair stiffen with horror at its unearthly and thrilling cadence.

We looked earnestly and eagerly in the direction from which the cry had seemed to proceed, but nothing was visible in that or, indeed, in any other direction.

The sun had set, and the grey of evening was deepening over the glassy surface of the water; but there was still light enough reflected from the sky to have enabled us to see any object within sight almost as distinctly as in broad day, but not an object of any description could we see, not even a solitary albatross.

We had carefully scanned, as far as was possible, the entire visible surface of the ocean, and had turned inquiringly towards each other, when once more rang out that mysterious cry, this time apparently close under our stern.

We turned, unutterably horror-stricken, in that direction, but there was *nothing*.   Seamen are, as a rule, as brave as lions ; but anything mysterious and unaccountable completely cowes them, and such, I confess, was now the case with us.

The cry was too sharp and loud to have proceeded from any distance ; and there was no visible explanation of it.   It was not repeated a third time, I am happy to say ; and I wish never to hear anything like it again.   What it was, or whence it came, we never knew, and I was, and am to this day, utterly unable to account for it.

I have since been informed that such sounds have occasionally been heard at sea by others as well as ourselves, but never with the result of any discovery as to their origin.

During the next three days we had nothing but light variable winds, and calms.

On the morning of the fourth day, at daybreak, we made a sail directly ahead.   At this time we had a nice little breeze, and were going about six knots.

As we neared her, we noticed that she was
hove-to, her courses brailed up, and her topgallant
yards on the caps.   When close to her, it struck
us that something must be the matter on board,
for not a soul could we see about her decks.   The
vessel herself too —a full-rigged ship of about fourteen hundred tons—struck us as being unusually
deep in the water.   There being no sea on, we
decided to run alongside and board her, thinking
she might possibly prove derelict.   We did so,
accordingly, rounding to under her stern, and
ranging up alongside on her lee quarter ; having
first, however, taken in our gaff-topsail and lowered
our topmast, so as not to foul her rigging.

As we came gently alongside, an exclamation
escaped Bob, who was standing forward, ready to
heave a line on board or jump up the side with it,
according to circumstances.

" Here's been some cursed foul play here, by
the look of it, Harry," exclaimed he; "mutiny and
murder, I should judge, by this," pointing to the
scuppers of the ship, from which blood had evidently been flowing, large semi-coagulated gouts
still adhering to the sides of the vessel, and about

the mouths of the scupper-holes.   The vessel
being, as I have said, very low in the water, we
had no difficulty whatever in boarding her; both
springing up the side at the same moment, each
with the end of a line in our hands.

Good heavens! what a sight met our horrified
gaze as we leaped down upon the ship's deck!

Some three or four and twenty corpses lay
there, with the blood still slowly oozing in a few
instances from wounds in various parts of their
bodies.

The wounds were mostly inflicted by cutlasses
and pistol-shots; but two of the bodies, apparently
those of officers, had the heads almost severed
from the trunks, the gashes having been evidently
inflicted by a keener weapon than a ship's cut-
lass.   These bodies had the arms lashed tightly
behind the back.

Too horror-stricken to speak a word, I walked
aft, Bob following me, and entered the cabin,
which was on deck, and from which I thought I
heard a groan issuing.   On entering, the first
object I saw was the body of a young man, about
four and twenty years of age, lying close across

the doorway, and covered with wounds. His left
arm was almost completely cut through; a long
gash had laid his forehead open from above the
right temple to the left eyebrow; a pistol-bullet
had entered his forehead nearly fair between the
eyes; and blood had evidently flowed copiously
from his right breast. This body lay across
three others, dressed in the usual attire of seamen.

On a sofa, which stretched entirely across the
after-part of the cabin, lay the body of a young
and most beautiful girl, her night-dress torn to
shreds, and her fair skin disfigured by deep blue
marks, and smeared with blood, indicating but too
clearly that she had been the victim of most
atrocious outrages.

And lastly, under the cabin table, lay another
body, from which, whilst we stood gazing in
speechless horror at these evidences of diabolical
atrocity, a faint groan issued.

Bob assisted me to draw the sufferer from
under the table; and we then saw that he was an
old man, grey-haired, and dressed in fine blue
cloth garnished with gilt buttons, and a stripe of

gold lace round the cuffs of the jacket; no doubt the master of the vessel.

Bob drew the corpse of the young girl somewhat aside, spreading the table-cover over the body reverently, to hide the naked limbs; and then, between us, we placed the wounded man on the sofa.

The cabin had, notwithstanding the ghastly appearance it presented, been the scene of a wild carouse, for the table was covered with glasses and wine and spirit bottles, and broken bottles and glasses littered the floor. I searched among the contents of the table until I found a bottle only partly empty, and from this I poured out a glass of its contents, which proved to be port, and managed with considerable difficulty to get a small quantity of the wine down the wounded man's throat. The skylight was open, and the air coming down through it in a cool gentle breeze, assisted the wine in restoring him to consciousness. He opened his eyes, and gazed round him vacantly for a moment or so, and then memory returned, and he burst violently into tears. We soothed him as well as we could, assuring him that we were friends, and that we would not leave him ; and in a minute or two he recovered strength and composure enough to speak.

" Thank you, gentlemen, thank you," said he, " but my time here is very short, and your well-meant efforts for my relief are not only useless, but they also increase my suffering. You are, I presume, from some ship which has come up with us since those fiends left. Kindly prop me up a little higher on the sofa, gentlemen, if you please, and I will endeavour to tell you what has happened before I pass away."

We did so ; and as we were making his position as easy as we could for him, his eye fell upon the body of the young girl, and once more his tears burst forth, mingled with prayers for her, and the most bitter curses upon her destroyers.

He raised one hand to his face as though to brush his tears away, and we then noticed for the first time—horror upon horror !—that his fingers had all been cut, or rather *hacked* out, at the knuckle-joints, the wounds still slowly bleeding.

He saw our looks of compassion, and said, as if in reply :

" Ah, gentlemen, willingly would I have submitted to be torn limb from limb by the demons, had they but spared my poor Rose—my darling, my only daughter."

After another short pause, he began :

" It was about midnight, last night, that we noticed a sail ahead of us, which was duly reported. There was not very much wind at the time, and she did not near us until about six bells. As she closed with us, her movements became so suspicious that I ordered the arm-chest on deck, called all hands, and served out the pistols and cutlasses to them.

" Our suspicions were very shortly confirmed, for when she was within a cable's length of us she sheered suddenly alongside, and about fifty men leaped from her on to our deck. Our poor fellows gave them a warm reception ; but they were all quickly cut down, and in about three minutes the pirates had the ship. They immediately began to plunder her, and a band of the most ruffianly of them, headed by their captain, made for the cabin. "Seeing that all was lost, my son—his body lies at the door there—and I rushed in here, to make a desperate stand in defence of my daughter.

"The poor fellow killed three of them, whilst I severely wounded others; but he was shot down, and I fell, exhausted with the wounds I had already received. My poor girl was soon discovered and dragged from her berth.

"The chief then questioned me as to our cargo, where we were from, and so on; and believing that treasure was concealed somewhere in the ship, he mutilated me thus," holding up his finger-less hands, "to force me to reveal its hiding-place. We had none, but he would not be convinced; and finding bodily torture of no avail to extract from me the information it was not in my power to give, the monster—oh, gentlemen! my poor, poor girl, my innocent, my gentle Rose—I *cannot* say it.

"Thank God! she soon died—of shame and a broken heart, doubtless; for even *they* seemed un-willing to stain their weapons with her blood. Would that they *had;* would that *I* had been able

so to steel my heart as to have slain her, rather
than that I should have seen what I did; for they
first bound me, and then placed me so that I could
see all. As soon as they found that she was
dead, they ransacked the cabin, turned out the
lockers, and drank and sang, until the mate, I
suppose, of the pirate came in and reported that
everything of value was transferred to the brig;
when the leader—whom I once or twice heard
addressed as Johnson "—Bob and I started and
looked at each other expressively—" ordered the
ship to be scuttled, and for all hands but those
employed on the work to return to the brig.
They then left the cabin; and, about half an hour
afterwards, I believe, they left the ship. She
cannot—float ver—very much—longer; but I
shall—shall be—gone before——"

His voice had been gradually growing weaker
and weaker as he approached the end of his
narrative, and now failed altogether. I tore
open the front of his shirt to ascertain if his heart
still beat, and now saw that he had received,
in addition to other wounds, a shot through the
chest.

There was no blood; but he, no doubt, bled internally. I could detect not the faintest flutter of the heart, so we laid him gently down on the sofa. As we did so, a small stream of blood trickled out of his mouth, he sighed heavily, and his jaw dropped.

Seeing that he was dead, we left the cabin, and stepped out once more into the bright sunshine. We noticed that, even during the short time we had been on board, the vessel had settled considerably in the water.

It was evidently quite time we were off; but we first went all round the deck, examining carefully each body, to see if either exhibited the least sign of life; but all were utterly beyond the reach of our help. We accordingly cast off, and returned on board the *Water Lily*, making all the sail we could, to get as speedily as possible away from the scene of such diabolical atrocities.

We were about four miles distant from the ship, when we observed her roll once or twice slowly and heavily; her stern rose, and, her bows disappearing beneath the water, she gradually became almost perpendicular, when she paused for a moment and then sank gently out of sight.

The moment that Johnson's name was mentioned, the same idea flashed into both our minds; that this was the same man, and probably the same ship, of which we had so lately heard. The captain spoke of the pirate vessel as a brig; and we felt no manner of doubt that she was the *Albatross*.

So then these men, the men who had showed such base treachery to my father, were still at large, and in full prosecution of their villanous designs. And not only so, but they were in the same quarter of the globe as ourselves, and manifestly at no very great distance.

We felt no difficulty whatever now in attaching a very different and much more sinister significance to the charred fragments of wreck we had lately passed. Our little craft would of course be but a poor prize to these rascals; but since they seemed so to luxuriate in cruelty it behoved us to give them as wide a berth as possible.

The presence of this craft, and that, too, in our immediate vicinity, was a source of the greatest anxiety to us; so much so, that we took in our gaff-topsail, and housed our topmast, to show but a low spread of canvas; and one or other of us remained posted at the mast-head all day, on the look-out, so as, if possible, to sight her before being seen ourselves, should it happen that we were both proceeding in the same direction, or on such courses as would bring us together.

We maintained this ceaseless watch for the pirate brig for four days, when, judging from the experience we had already obtained of our sailing powers in fine weather as compared with those of other vessels that we had fallen in with, we came to the conclusion that all immediate danger of a *rencontre* with her was past; and we accordingly relaxed our vigilance, and allowed ourselves some rest, which, by this time, we greatly needed.

About noon on the seventh day after boarding the ship scuttled by the pirates (the name of which I forgot to mention was the *Massachusetts*, of New York), land appeared ahead. It was the Falkland group of barren and desolate islands in the vicinity of Cape Horn. As we had been expecting, the wind now drew round from the westward, fresh, though not so much so as to prevent our showing a jib-headed gaff-topsail to it.

Under this sail the little *Water Lily* made most excellent way; going a good eight knots through the water, close hauled, and against a very respectable head sea. As the day drew on, the wind freshened ; and, though we carried on as long as we dared, wishing to get round the dreaded Cape as quickly as possible, we were obliged at sunset to take our topsail in, in order to save our topmast.

By breakfast-time next morning it became necessary to further reduce our canvas, and we accordingly took down a reef in our mainsail. The question now arose whether it would be better to go round outside of everything, or to attempt the Straits of Magellan. We hove the little craft to, and went below and carefully examined the chart ; discussing, as we did so, the comparative advantages and disadvantages of the two routes.

Bob had experience of both; and he seemed to feel that in the present state of the weather, and with the wind as it was, we were likely to make a quicker passage by going on to the southward, and passing round the Horn. I was of the same opinion, by no means liking the intricacies of the navigation of the Straits, or the violent tides which our sailing directions told us swept through them.

We accordingly filled away again, carrying on, notwithstanding the still freshening breeze, until the little *Water Lily* seemed alternately to threaten diving to the bottom with us or taking flight altogether into the air. We were nearly blinded by the copious showers of spray which flew over us, and our mainsail was wet to its very peak; yet it was a real pleasure to see the ease and lightness with which the boat skimmed over the now formidable and angry sea.

About four bells in the morning watch, we passed within three miles of the easternmost end of Staten Island. An hour later, the breeze freshened upon us so fiercely that we saw it would be dangerous to trifle with it any longer; so we hauled down our mainsail and stowed it; and bent and set the trysail in its place, single reefed. This change proved a very great relief to the little craft, the sway and leverage of the heavy main-boom having made her plunge tremendously;

whereas, now, she went along without shipping a drop of water beyond the spray which she of course still continued to throw over herself.

It was whilst we were busy shifting our after canvas that the little *Lily* experienced perhaps one of the most narrow escapes of the whole voyage. We were too much occupied with our work to keep a very bright look-out; indeed, we considered that, beyond the state of the weather, there was nothing to demand our attention.

We had just completed the bending of the try-sail, when away to windward of us, not more than a quarter of a mile distant, we observed a large ship running down directly upon us before the wind, under top-gallant stunsails.

The *Lily* was almost stationary at the time; and the ship was heading as straight as she possibly could for us. How the trysail went up, it is impossible for me to say; we pulled like demons, and it seemed to rise instantaneously into its place, fully set. I sprang aft, and put the helm hard up, to gather way; and we had just begun to draw through the water, when the ship took a sheer as though to cross our bows. I kept the tiller

jammed hard over, and eased away the trysail
sheet, intending to wear; when the ship took
another sheer directly towards us.

She was now close aboard of us, and not a soul
could I see on the look-out. Bob rushed aft,
with his eye on the ship's bowsprit, evidently prepared for a spring; whilst I shifted the tiller and
flattened in the trysail sheet once more. That
saved us. The cutter luffed just in time, and
shot literally from beneath the ship's bows. So
close were we, that had the stranger been *pitching*
instead of *'scending* at the moment, her jibboom-
end must have passed through the peak of our
trysail.

It may seem to the uninitiated an easy matter
to keep out of an approaching ship's way, by simply observing the precise direction in which she is
steering; but, as a matter of fact, a ship, when
running before the wind, sails in anything but a
straight line, *sheering* first one way and then
another, and it is quite impossible for a spectator
to judge with accuracy in which direction she will
sheer at a given moment; hence the danger in
which we so unexpectedly found ourselves.

CHAPTER IX.

A CAPE HORN GALE.

WE stood on to the southward and westward during the remainder of that day, the wind continuing still to freshen, and the sea getting up with most fearful rapidity. The glass fell slowly too, and there appeared to be every prospect of our getting a taste of the quality of the weather for which Cape Horn is so notorious.

As the sun set, the veil of cloud-wrack which had obscured the heavens all day was rent asunder in the western quarter, and we caught a glimpse of the great luminary hanging upon the verge of the horizon like a ball of molten copper.

His level beams shot for a few moments across

the broad expanse of the heaving and wildly-leaping waters, tinging the wave-crests immediately in his wake with deep blood-red, whilst all around elsewhere the angry ocean was darkest indigo. A few rays shot upward, gleaming wiidly among the flying scud, and then the orb of day sank into the ocean, shooting abroad as he did so a sudden baleful crimson glare, which gradually died out in the gloom of increasing storm and coming night.

Bob stood by my side watching the wild scene I have so feebly described, and as the sun disappeared, he turned to me and remarked :

" My eyes, Harry ! what d'ye think of that, lad ? To my mind it needs no prophet to tell us with that afore our eyes that we're booked for a reg'lar thorough-bred Cape Horn gale of wind ; and my advice as chief-mate of this here barkie is, that we makes her just as snug as we knows how, for, depend upon it, afore morning we shall have as thorough a trial of her sea-goin' qualities as we're likely to want for many a day to come."

" My own idea, Bob," replied I ; " I have

seldom seen a wilder sunset, and if it does not
mean wind, and plenty of it too, all my weather-
lore must go for nothing, and I shall have to turn
to and learn everything over afresh."

"Ay, ay! you may say that," returned he,
" and I the same ; but we've both knocked about
too many years at sea to make any mistake in
our reading when Natur' opens so plain a page
of her book for us as yond ; so the sooner we
turns to the better, say I, or we shall have the
darkness upon us afore we're ready for it.   Thank
God, we've plenty of sea-room ; so let's rouse
up that floating-anchor contrivance of yourn, my
lad, for, depend upon it, if ever the *Lily* is likely
to need the consarn she will to-night."

This floating-anchor I will describe for the
benefit of those who may not have seen such a
thing, for it is a most useful affair, and no small
craft should undertake a long cruise without one.
Ours was formed of two flat bars of iron, each ten
feet in length, riveted together in the centre in
such a way that they would either fold flat one
upon the other (for convenience of stowage), or

open out at right angles, forming a cross of four equal arms.

In each end of each bar was a hole capable of taking a good stout rope swifter, which was set up taut when the bars were opened, so as to keep them spread at right angles. Four other holes were punched, two in each bar, about midway between each end and the centre rivet; these were for the reception of a crowfoot.

As soon as the bars were spread open, and the swifter passed and set up, a square sheet of the stoutest canvas, painted, was spread over them, the edges laced to the swifter with a stout lacing, and the crowfoot toggled through the intermediate holes in the bars and corresponding holes in the canvas.

A buoy was then attached to the end of one arm to float the anchor, with a sufficient amount of buoy-rope to allow it to sink to the requisite depth; the end of the cable was shackled into the thimble of the crowfoot, the buoy streamed over-board, and the anchor let go.

I may as well state here, that for the econo-misation of space the buoy for floating our anchor was an india-rubber ball, made of the same materials as an ordinary air-cushion, and distended in the same way. This was enclosed in a strong net of three-strand sinnet, which net was attached to the buoy-rope.

We hove the craft to whilst we were preparing the anchor, and glad enough was I when it was ready; for by this time the sea was running so high and breaking so heavily that I was afraid once or twice, when we were caught broadside-to, that we should be capsized.

We let go the anchor with only two fathoms of buoy-rope, so as to sink it just deep enough to keep us head to sea without materially interfering with the craft's drift, as we thought we should ride all the easier for such an arrangement, and so it proved.

As soon as the anchor was let go, we got our head-sail in, ran in the bowsprit, and got our topmast on deck; the trysail was close-reefed, and the sheet trimmed amidships, the anchor-light hoisted well up on the fore-stay, and our preparations for the night were complete.

By this time it was blowing tremendously

heavy, and the howling of the gale overhead, the shriek of the wind through our scanty rigging, and the hiss of the foaming water around us mingled into such a deafening sound that Bob and I had fairly to *shout*, even when close alongside of each other, to make ourselves heard. And then it began to thunder and lighten heavily, still further increasing the wild and impressive grandeur of the scene upon which we gazed in awe-struck admiration.

At one moment all would be deep black pitchy night, lighted up only by the pale unearthly shimmer of some foaming wave-crest as it rolled menacingly down upon us, gleaming with phosphorescent light; anon the canopy above would be rent asunder by the vivid lightning-flash, and for an instant the vast whirling forms of the torn and shredded clouds would be revealed, with a momentary vision of the writhing, leaping, and storm-driven waters beneath them, illumined by the ghastly glare of the levin-brand, and stricken into sudden rigidity by the rapidity of the flash.

We stayed on deck for about an hour after our

anchor was let go, watching this grand manifestation of the power of the Deity, sublime as terrible,
terrible as sublime; and then, finding that no
improvement suggested itself in our arrangements,
and that the *Lily* rode like a cork over the moun-
tain-billows—though occasionally the comb of a
more than usually heavy sea would curl in over
the bows and send a foaming cataract of water aft
and out over her taffrail—we descended to the
cabin to get our suppers, for which, by this time,
we were quite ready.

So easy was the motion of the little craft that
when we got below we found no difficulty whatever in boiling the water, and making ourselves a
cup of good strong tea. While discussing this
refreshing beverage and a few biscuits, we arrived
at the conclusion that as we had done all it was
possible to do for the safety of the boat, it was
useless to keep a watch through the night, and
that we would, therefore, take advantage of the
opportunity to get a good undisturbed night's rest,
leaving the "sweet little cherub that sits up aloft"
to look out.

Accordingly, as soon as our meal was over, I

left Bob to straighten up below, while I went on deck to take a last look round and see that everything was snug and as it should be, and our light burning brightly.

I found everything satisfactory, except that it seemed to be blowing harder than ever; however I could not help that, so I went below again, closing the companion after me; and we both turned in, chatted awhile, listened to the roaring of the gale and the occasional heavy wash of water along the deck, and finally dropped off to sleep.

I awoke two or three times during the night, and once I turned out and pushed the slide of the companion far enough back to put my head outside; but the night was still as black as pitch, it was blowing harder if anything than before, and the air was full of spindrift and scudwater; so I pushed over the slide again, and tumbled once more into my comfortable hammock, very vividly impressed both with a sense of our helplessness in the midst of such a heavy gale, and also with the comparative degrees of comfort between the decks and the cabin.

Bob was the first to make a muster in the morning; and his first act, like mine during the night, was to take a look out upon deck.

"Blowing hard enough to blow the devil's horns off," I heard him exclaim, "and as thick as a hedge. And, my precious eyes! what a sea! come up and take a look at it, Harry, boy; I never see'd nothing like it all the years I've been afloat. Hurrah, young un! *that's* your sort," as the cutter rose fearfully near to the perpendicular in surmounting the crest of a sea, and then slid down, down, down into the trough, until it seemed as though she would sink to the very ocean's bed. "And *don't* the little hussy behave beautifully! She's as floaty as a gull, Hal; and drier than e'er a seventy-four that ever was launched would be in a sea like this. Now, what lubber comes here with his eyes sealed up instead of looking before him? Jump up, Harry; quick, boy! we are in a mess here, and no mistake. No, no; it's all right, he'll clear us a'ter all. No thanks to him though, for there's not a soul—ah! so you're beginning to wake up at last, eh!"

Here I put my head up through the companion, alongside of Bob's lovely phiz, and saw within forty fathoms of us, over the ridge of a sea, and broad on our port beam, the topmast-heads of a brig. As we both rose together on the same sea, her sails first, and then her hull, came into view.

She was not a large vessel ; about two hundred tons or thereabouts, apparently ; painted all black down to her copper, excepting a narrow red ribbon which marked the line of her sheer.

She was hove to on the port tack under a storm - staysail, and her topgallant - masts were down on deck. Everything was very trim and man-o'-war-like on board her ; but no government dockyard ever turned out such a beautiful model as she was.

When I first caught sight of her, she was heading directly for us ; but as we watched her, her head paid off, and she swept slowly down across our stern, near enough for us to have hove a biscuit on board her.

Some ten or a dozen heads peered curiously at us over her weather bulwarks as she drove slowly past us, and one man aft on the quarter-deck, the officer of the watch apparently, seized a trumpet to hail us; but whether he did so or not, or, if he did, what he said, we neither of us knew; for at that moment we both sank once more into the trough with a perfect mountain of water between us, until we lost sight of him altogether for a moment, even to his mast-heads.

I took the glass, which we always kept slung in beckets in the companion-way, open and adjusted ready for immediate use, and as she rose once more into view I applied it to my eye, and the first thing which caught my attention was her name, painted on her stern, which was now towards us.

"The *Albatross*, by all that's unlucky!" exclaimed I.

"Blest if we mightn't have guessed as much if we'd been in a guessin' humour," ejaculated Bob. "Honest-going merchant ships ain't so plaguy careful of their spars as that chap—leastways, not such small fry as he is. Pity but what they was, I often says; but where d'ye find a skipper who'll be bothered to send down his top hamper every time it pipes up a bit of a breeze? No; 'Let it stand if 'twill,' is the word, 'and if 'twon't, let it blow away.' But the chap is a real good seaman, Harry, no man'll deny that ; look how snug he's got everything ; and all hauled taut and coiled down neat and reg'lar man-o'-war fashion I'll be bound."

We got, I think, a clearer idea of the tremendous strength of the gale by watching the brig than we did even by the motions of our own little craft. She was tossed about like the merest cockleshell, and every time that she rose upon the crest of a sea, the wind took her rag of a staysail, distending it as though it would tear it clean out of the boltropes, and heeling the vessel over until we could see the whole of her bottom nearly down to her keel ; and then her sharp bows would cleave the wave-crest in a perfect cataract of foam and spray, and away she would settle down once more with a heavy weather-roll into the trough.

"Well," exclaimed Bob, as we lost sight of her in the driving scud, " she's a pretty sea-boat is yon brig ; but I'm blest if the little *Lily* don't beat her even at that game. What say you, Harry ;

ain't she proving true the very words I spoke that night when we first began to talk about this here v'yage?"

"Indeed she is, Bob," I answered; "I am as surprised as I am delighted at her behaviour; I could never have believed, without seeing it myself, that so small a craft would even live in such weather, much less be as comfortable as she is. But I don't like *that*," continued I, as the comb of a tremendous sea came curling in over our bows, fairly smothering the little craft in foam for a moment, though she came up immediately afterwards, "shaking her feathers" like a duck. "I'm afraid one of these gentlemen will be starting our skylight or companion for us; and that would be a very serious matter."

"Never fear," returned Bob confidently. "Our bit of a windlass and the mast breaks the force of it before it reaches the skylight. And that idee of yours in having it rounded at the fore end is a capital one; it turns the water off each side almost like the stem of a ship, besides bein' stronger than a square-shaped consarn. At the same time, all this water coming in on deck don't do no *good*

if it don't do no *harm;* but how's it to be per-
vented ?"

" I have an idea," said I, "and it's worth a trial.
It can do no harm, and if it fails we are no worse
off than we were before."

So saying, I dived below and got out a bottle
of oil, through the cork of which I bored three or
four holes with a corkscrew, but left the cork in.
To the neck of the bottle I made fast the end of
about a fathom of marline, and then, going forward, I made fast the other end of the marline to
one of the links of the chain-cable by which we
were riding to our floating-anchor.

I then sung out to Bob to give her a few
fathoms more chain, and as he did so I hove the
bottle overboard.

In about five minutes the success of my experiment became manifest. The oil leaked slowly out
through the holes I had bored in the cork, and,
diffusing itself on the surface of the water, caused
the seas to sweep by us either without breaking
at all, or, if they *did* break, it was with such
diminished force that no more water came on
board.

I had heard of "oil on troubled waters" before, but at the time that I did so I never expected to put its virtues to so thoroughly practical a test.

We went below and got breakfast under weigh; and whilst discussing the meal, our conversation naturally turned upon the appearance of the *Albatross*.

"There can be no question, I fear, as to its being that scoundrel Johnson and his gang of desperadoes," said I, half hoping to hear Bob dispute the probability.

But he was quite of my opinion.

"No, no," said he, "that's the scamp, never a doubt of it. *I* noticed the name on his starn; but there warn't no name of a port where he hails from, for the simple reason that he hails from nowhere in particular. Besides, a man with half an eye could tell by looking at that craft that she's strong handed. Depend on't, Harry, there's too many hammocks in her fo'c'stle for an honest trader. And, worst luck, she's bound the same road as ourselves— at least, she's going round the Horn; but a'ter she gets round it's not so easy to say what course she may steer. We must hope she's on the look-out for some stray Spaniard or other coming down the coast; for if we falls in with her ag'in, she'll have some'at to say to us, mark my words."

"You surely do not suppose the man will condescend to give such a pigmy as ourselves a thought, do you?"

"That's just what he's doing at this identical moment, it's my opinion," returned Bob. "He is not fool enough to suppose we're down here somewheres off the Horn, in this cockle-shell, on a pleasure trip; and that we're not come down here to trade he also knows pretty well, or we should have a craft big enough to stow away something like a paying cargo; and if we're here for neither one nor t'other of them objects, he'll want to know what we *are* here for; and, depend upon it, he won't be happy till he's found out. So take my advice, Harry, and, if we fall in with him again, let's give him a wide berth."

"Decidedly; I shall do so if possible," returned I. "But that may prove no such easy matter with so smart a vessel as he has under his feet."

"Not in heavy weather, certainly," said Bob;

"but give us weather in which we can carry a topsail, even if it's no more nor a jib-header, and I'll say,

Catch who catch can!' Why, we can lay a good two p'ints closer to the wind than he can, and still keep a good clean full; and the square-rigged craft that can beat us in going to wind'ard must be an out-and-out flyer, and no mistake. We must keep a bright look-out, and not be caught napping, that's all; and give *everything* a good wide berth till we're pretty certain of what it is."

"Well," said I, "I trust we shall not fall in with him again. The Pacific is a pretty big place, and it's not so easy to find a craft in it when you don't know where to look for her. If we *do* meet with him again, we must do all we can to avoid him, and hope for the best."

"Ay, ay," returned Bob, "'hope for the best and prepare for the worst' is a good maxim for any man. It takes him clear of many a difficulty, and enables him to lay his course on the v'yage of life clean full, and with slack bowlines. As for this here Johnson, I'd ask nothing better than to have him just out of gun-shot under our lee, with a nice breeze, and not too much sea for the little

Lily, and then let him catch us if he's man enough for the job."

I certainly could not echo this wish of Bob's; but it was satisfactory to find that he had such great confidence in the boat and in her ability to escape from the *Albatross*, so I allowed him to remain in undisturbed enjoyment of his own opinion, especially as it seemed to afford him considerable entertainment, and went on deck to take another look at the weather.

There was no sign of the gale breaking; in fact it seemed to be scarcely at its height, for away to windward it looked as dirty and as full of wind as ever; and the sea was something awful to contemplate. It looked, of course, worse to us than it would to those on the deck of a large ship; but even allowing for that, it was unquestionably running far higher than anything I had ever seen before.

I have read somewhere that scientific men assert that even in the heaviest gales and in mid-ocean the sea never attains a greater height than twenty feet from trough to crest; but with all due respect to them and their science-founded opinions, I take leave to assert that they are in this instance mistaken.

An intelligent sailor (and I modestly claim to be at least this much) is as capable of judging the height of a sea as the most scientific of mortals; and I am confident of this, that *many* of the seas I watched that morning ran as high as our cross-trees, which were a trifle over thirty feet above the surface of the water.

Indeed, to satisfy myself *thoroughly* upon this point I climbed so high (with the utmost difficulty, and at very great risk of being blown overboard), and whilst looking over the crosstrees, I saw the crest of more than one sea rearing itself between my eye and the horizon.

So far the *Water Lily* had weathered the gale scatheless; there was not so much as a ropeyarn out of its place or carried away; and as there seemed to be no greater danger than there had been through the night, and as I had taken a good look round when aloft without seeing anything, we both went below to enjoy the comfort of the cabin, for on deck everything was cold, wet, and dismal in the extreme.

I was anxious to get a sight of the sun at noon, if possible, so as to ascertain our exact latitude. I knew we were not very far to the southward of Staten ; and I did not know but there might be a current setting us toward it, in which case we might find ourselves very awkwardly situated.

It looked half inclined to break away two or three times during the morning ; but as mid-day approached it became as bad as ever ; and I had the vexation of seeing noon pass by without so much as a momentary glimpse of the sun.

Towards evening, therefore, I took advantage of an exceptionally clear moment, and again scrambled aloft and took a thorough good look all round, and especially to the northward. There was nothing in sight ; and with this I was obliged to rest satisfied.

We noticed just about this time that the seas were beginning to break on board again, so I concluded that our bottle of oil was exhausted, and accordingly got out another, and having bored holes in the cork, as I had done with the first, it was bent on to the cable, more cable paid out, and we again rode all the easier. Our anchor-light was trimmed and lighted and hoisted up, and we went below to our tea, or *supper*, as sailors generally term it.

We had found the day dreadfully tedious, cooped up as we were in our low cabin, and a meal was a most welcome break in the monotony. We sat long over this one, therefore, prolonging it to its utmost extent ; and when it was over, we both turned to and cleared up the wreck.

By the time that all was done it was intensely dark ; but, before settling down below for the night, we both put our heads up through the companion, to take a last look round.

Bob was rather beforehand with me, and he had no sooner put his head outside than he pulled it in again, exclaiming, in an awe-struck tone :

" Look here, Harry ; what d'ye think of this ?"

I looked in the direction he indicated, and there upon our lowermast-head, and also upon the try-sail gaff-end, was a globe of pale, sickly green light, which wavered to and fro, lengthening out and flattening in again as the cutter tossed wildly over the mountainous seas.

It had not the appearance of flame, but rather

of highly luminous mist, brilliant at the core, and softening off and becoming more dim as the circumference of the globe was reached ; and it emitted a feeble and unearthly light of no great power.

I had never seen such a thing before, but I had often heard of it, and I recognised our strange visitors at once as *corposants*, or " lamps of St. Elmo," as they are called by the seamen of the Mediterranean ; though our own sailors call them by the less dignified name of " Davy Jones' lanterns."

" What d'ye think of bein' boarded by the likes of that ?" again queried Bob, in a hoarse whisper. " Old Davy is out on a cruise to-night, I reckon ; and it looks as though he meant to pay *us* a visit, by his h'isting them two lanterns of his'n in our rigging. Did ye ever see anything like it afore, Harry, lad ?"

" Never," replied I, " but I have often heard them spoken of, old man ; and though they certainly *are* rather queer to look at, they are easily accounted for. I have heard it said that they are the result of a peculiar electrical condition of the atmosphere, and that the electricity, attracted by any such points as the yard-arms or mast-heads of a ship, accumulates there until it becomes visible in the form we are now looking at."

" And is the light never visible except at the end of a spar ?" queried Bob.

" I believe not," I replied ; " but———"

" Then sail ho !" exclaimed Bob excitedly, pointing in the direction of our starboard bow.

I looked in the direction he indicated, but was too late : we were on the very summit of a wave at the moment that Bob spoke, but were now settling into the trough. As we rose to the next sea, however, I not only saw the ghostly light, but also got an indistinct view of the ship herself.

She was fearfully close, but appeared to be at the moment sheering away from us. She looked long enough for a three-masted vessel, but one mast only was standing, evidently the mainmast. The corposant appeared to have attached itself to the stump of her foremast, which had been carried away about fifteen or twenty feet from the deck ; and I thought her bowsprit seemed also to be missing.

She was scudding under close-reefed maintop-sail, and, from her sluggish movements, was evidently very much overloaded, or, what I thought more probable, had a great deal of water in her. I was the more inclined to this opinion from the peculiar character of her motions.

As she rose on the back of a sea, her stern seemed at first to be *pinned down*, as it were, until it appeared as though the following wave would run clean over her ; but gradually her stern rose until it was a considerable height above the water, whilst her bow in its turn seemed weighed down, as would be the case with a large body of water rushing from aft forward.

They evidently saw our light, for a faint hail of "—— ahoy !" came down the wind to us from her.

" In distress and wants assistance, by the look of it," remarked Bob. " But, poor chaps, it's little of that we can give 'em. Heaven and 'arth ! look at that, Harry."

As he spoke, the ship, which was rushing forward furiously on the back of a sea, suddenly sheered wildly to port, until she lay broadside to ;

the crest of the sea overtook her, and, breaking on board her in one vast volume of wildly flashing foam, threw her down upon her beam-ends, and, as it swept over her, her mast declined more and more towards the water, until it lay submerged.

Then, as we gazed in speechless horror at the dreadful catastrophe, a loud, piercing shriek rang out clear and shrill above the hoarse diapason of the howling tempest. She rolled completely bottom upwards, and then disappeared.

" Broached to, and capsized!" ejaculated we both in the same breath.

" Jump below, Bob, and rouse up a coil of line, whilst I get the life-buoys ready," exclaimed I, after a single moment's pause to collect my scattered faculties.

In an instant I had all four of the buoys ready, and two of them bent on to the longest rope-ends I could lay my hands on, and, in another, that glorious Bob appeared with a coil of rat-line on his shoulder and a lighted blue-light in his hand.

The stops were cut and the ends of the coil cleared in no time, and the two remaining buoys bent on, while Bob held the blue light aloft at arm's length, for the double purpose of throwing the light as far as possible over the water, and also to indicate our whereabouts to any strong swimmer who might be struggling for his life among the mountain surges, and to guide him to our tiny ark of refuge.

For nearly an hour did we peer anxiously into the gloom, in the hope of seeing some poor soul within reach of such assistance as it was in our power to afford, but in vain; there is no doubt that the vessel sucked all hands down with her when she sank into her watery grave.

When at last we reluctantly desisted from our efforts, and were in the act of securing the life-buoys once more, Bob cast his eyes aloft, and called my attention to the fact that the corpo-sants had disappeared.

"Depend on't, Harry," quoth he, "them lan-terns didn't come aboard of us for nothing. They mightn't have meant mischief for *us* exactly —for you can't always read Old Davy's signs aright; but you see they *did* mean mischief, and plenty of it too, for they no sooner appears aloft than a fine ship and her crew goes down close alongside of us ; and as soon as that bit of work was over, away they go somewhere else to light up the scene of further devilry, I make no manner of doubt."

It was utterly in vain that I attempted to argue the honest fellow out of his belief that their appearance was a portent of disaster, for his mind was deeply imbued with all those superstitious notions which appear to take such peculiarly firm hold on the ideas of sailors ; and against superstitions of lifelong duration, argument and reason are of but little avail.

As may readily be believed, our slumbers that night, after witnessing so distressing a scene, were anything but sound. Bob and I were up and down between the deck and the cabin at least half a dozen times before morning, and it was with a sense of unutterable relief that, as day broke, we found that the gale was breaking also.

By the time that breakfast was over there was a sensible diminution in the force of the wind, and by noon it cleared away sufficiently over-head to enable me to get an observation, not a particularly good one certainly—the sea was running far too high for that ; but it enabled me to ascertain that we were at least sixty miles to the southward of Staten.

About four p.m. I got a very much better observation for my longitude, and I found by it that our drift had not been anything like so great as I had calculated it would be. This I thought might possibly arise from our being in a weather-setting current.

There was still rather too much of both wind and sea to make us disposed to get under way that night, but we managed to get the craft up to the buoy of our floating-anchor, which we weighed and let go again with five fathoms of buoy-rope.

This was to prevent as much as possible any further drift to leeward, and to take full advantage of the current, the existence of which we suspected.

Next morning, however, the weather had so far moderated that, tired of our long inaction, we resolved to make a start once more, so shaking the reefs out of the trysail, and rigging our bowsprit out far enough to set a small jib, we got our floating-anchor in, and stood away to the southward and westward, with the wind out from . about west-nor'-west.

CHAPTER X.

THE weather now rapidly became finer, and the ocean, no longer lashed into fury by the breath of the tempest, subsided once more into long regular undulations. The wind hauled gradually more round from the northward too, and blew warm and balmy; a most welcome change after the raw and chilly weather we had lately experienced.

We once more cracked on sail upon the little *Water Lily;* and on the morning following that upon which we filled away upon our course, finding by observation that we were well clear of the Cape, and that we had plenty of room even should the wind once more back round from the

westward, we hauled close-up, and stood away on
a nor'-west-and-by-westerly course.

Nothing of importance occurred for more than
a week. The weather continued settled, and the
glass stood high; the wind was out at about
north, and sufficiently moderate to permit of
our carrying our jib-headed topsail; and day
after day we flew forward upon our course,
seldom making less than ten knots in the
hour, and occasionally reaching as high as
thirteen.

We were perfectly jubilant; for having rounded
the Cape in safety we now considered our troubles
over and our ultimate success as certain. We
were fairly in the Pacific, the region of fine
weather; and our little barkie had behaved so
well in the gale that our confidence in her sea-
worthiness was thoroughly established; so that all
fear of future danger from bad weather was completely taken off our minds.

One morning, the wind having fallen considerably lighter during the preceding night, as soon
as breakfast was over I roused up our square-

headed topsail, with the intention of setting it in the room of the small one.

But when I proceeded to take the latter in, I found that the halliards were somehow jammed aloft, and I shinned up to clear them. No sailor, if he really be a *seaman*, and not a tinker or a tailor, ever goes aloft without taking a good look round him ; so after I had cleared the halliards I clung to the slim spar for a minute or two whilst I swept the horizon carefully around.

" Sail ho !" shouted I, as I caught a glimpse of the royals of a vessel gleaming snowy white in the brilliant sunshine far away in the south-western board.

" Where away ?" shouted Bob.

" Broad on our lee-bow," I answered, still clinging to the thin wire-topmast shrouds.

" What d'ye make her out to be, Harry, my lad ?" was the next question.

" Either a barque or a brig," answered I ; " the latter I am inclined to believe, though he is still too far away for his mizzen-mast to show, if he has one."

"Why d'ye think it's a brig, Harry?" queried Bob.

" His canvas looks too small for that of a barque," replied I, as I slid down on deck, having seen all that it was possible to see at present.

" Then it's that —— *Albatross* again, for a thousand," ejaculated Bob in a tone of deep disgust. " That's just the p'int where he might reasonably be looked for. He made sail long enough afore we did, a'ter the gale had blowed itself out, and consequently got a good long leg to the west'ard of us ; but as we've been steering perhaps a couple of p'ints higher than he has for most of the time since, we've overhauled him ; and now he's come round to go to the nor'ard, and we've fallen in with him once more."

I was inclined to take the same view of the matter that Bob did. It is true that when once a ship passes out of sight at sea you can never be sure of her exact position afterwards ; yet, under certain circumstances, taking the direction of the wind and the state of the weather as data upon which to base your argument, and, in conjunction with these, the course the vessel was steering when last seen, or the part of the world to which you have reason to believe she is bound, it is astonishing how near a guess may be and is not unfrequently made as to her whereabouts.

Now we knew that the *Albatross* was bound to the Pacific when we last saw her, because she was then hove-to, evidently with the intention of maintaining as weatherly a position as possible. Had she been bound to the eastward, the weather was not so bad at that time as to have prevented her scudding before it, which she undoubtedly would have done under such circumstances, making a fair wind of it.

At the same time there was of course a possibility of our being mistaken as to the craft in sight being the pirate-brig, it being by no means an unusual thing for vessels as small as she was, or even smaller, to venture round the Cape.

" Well," said I, " perhaps it will be safest, Bob, to assume for the present that this brig *is* the *Albatross*. What, under such circumstances, is your advice ?"

" Which of us has the weather-gage, d'ye think ?" queried Bob.

" It is rather difficult to decide at present," I replied. " Much depends upon which of us is the

fastest. If we are both going at about the same
speed, I should say we shall pass extremely close
to her."

" How is she heading, Harry ?" was the next
question.

" To the northward, rather edging down towards us, if anything," I thought.

" Ay, ay," chuckled Bob, " it ain't *every* craft
as can stick her bowsprit into the wind's eye like
this here little barkie. Now I dare swear he's
jammed hard up upon a taut bowline, and here *we*
are going as close to the wind as he is, and every
thread ramping full. Take hold of her a minute,
Hal, and let's see what these old eyes of mine can
tell us about the stranger."

I took hold of the tiller, and Bob went aloft
with the deliberation of the seaman who is in no
particular hurry. Having reached the crosstrees,
he stood upon them, with one hand grasping the
peak-halliards to steady himself, whilst with the
other he shaded his eyes.

" I see her, I see her," he exclaimed ; " we're
raising her fast, Harry, my boy ; and in another
half hour or so we shall see her from the deck."

He then went as high as the yard of the topsail, and clung there for a good five minutes, reading all the signs which a seaman sees in the almost imperceptible peculiarities of rig, shape of sails, etc. Having satisfied himself, he descended deliberately to the deck, evidently ruminating deeply.

" Now I'll tell ye what I think of the matter, Harry," said he, as he came aft and seated himself beside me. " There's a familiar sort of a look with that craft away yonder ; I seems to recognise her as some'at I've seen afore ; and I've no moral doubt in the world but what it's that villain Johnson, although we can't be *sartain* of it until we gets a nearer look at her. And I've an idee that, if anything, it's *we* that's got the weather-gage ; and if so, by all means keep it, even if we has to run the gauntlet of her broadside for a minute or two. Once let's be to wind'ard, and in such weather as this I wouldn't fear the smartest *square - rigged* craft that ever was launched. We could lead 'em no end of a dance, and then give 'em the slip a'terwards when we was tired of the fun. So *my* advice is to luff up as close as you can ; not *too* close ye know, lad ; let her go through it ; but spring your luff all as you can get, and let's try what our friend yonder is made of. As long as we're to *leeward* of him the game is *his ;* but let's get to *wind'ard* of him and it's *ours* to do what we like with it."

I had it in my mind to take in all the canvas and lie *perdu* until the brig had crossed our course and was well out of our road to the northward ; but that would still be leaving him the weather-gage ; and I saw fully as clearly as Bob did the advantage of obtaining this, if possible ; so on we stood, boldly, lying a good point higher than we had been before steering, yet keeping every sail a good clean full, and drawing to perfection.

The wind, however, was dropping fast ; and by the time that the sun was on the meridian we were not going more than five knots. This made me extremely anxious ; more particularly as the stranger proved a remarkably fast vessel ; so much so, that it still remained a matter of doubt which of us would cross the other.

Bob, on the other hand, was delighted beyond

measure, stoutly avowing that the falling breeze was little, if anything, short of a divine manifestation in our favour. He declared himself ready to stake all he was possessed of in the world (and if the brig should turn out to be the pirate, he actually *was* staking his life) on our speed as against that of the stranger in light winds, and was already chuckling in anticipation over that craft's discomfiture.

She was within about five miles of us, still maintaining her relative position of about four points on our lee bow, when Bob served dinner on deck, as was our custom in fine weather.

We were very busy with the viands, keeping one eye always on the brig however, when we noticed something fluttering over her taffrail; and the next moment a flag of some sort floated up to her peak.

I was at the tiller; so Bob took the glass, and levelling it at the brig, gave her a more thorough scrutiny than we had bestowed upon her at all hitherto.

"The stars and stripes, and a pennant!" exclaimed he, with his eye still at the tube.

" Lord bless us for the two pretty innocents he takes us for, Harry ; but there, of course he don't know as we've got his character and all about him at our fingers' ends. Well, anyhow, we won't be behindhand with him in the matter of politeness ;" and therewith Master Bob dived below, returning in a moment with our ensign and club burgee in his hand, which he bent to their respective halliards and ran them up—the one to our gaff-end, and the other to our masthead.

As we had by this time finished our meal, Bob cleared the things away, muttering something about having " plenty to do afore long besides eating and drinking."

Our colours had not been displayed above a minute, when four small balls were seen ascending to the brig's main royal-masthead, where they broke abroad and waved lazily out in the failing breeze as a signal.

Bob at once assumed the duties of signal-officer, by once more taking a peep through the glass.

" Commercial code pennant," said he ; and then he read out the flags beneath it.

" Run down and fetch up the signal-book,"
said I.

He did so ; we turned up the signal, and read,
" Come under my lee ; I wish to speak you."

" Thank 'ee !" ejaculated Bob, " not if we can
help it, Mister Johnson. I reckon 'twould be
about the most onprofitable conwersation as ever
the crew of this here cutter took a part in.
We've got our own wholesome planks to walk,
aboard here, when we wants any of that sort of
exercise ; and though there's not much to boast
of in the way of room, I dare say there's more
of *that* than we'd find on the plank *you*'d give
us for a parade ground. Seems to me, Hal, as
we're bringing him nearer abeam than he was a
while ago ; ain't it so ?"

" You are right, Bob," I replied, glancing at
the compass ; " he is more than a point farther
aft than he was a quarter of an hour ago ; but
is it not possible that we are giving ourselves
needless uneasiness ? That craft certainly has a
look of the *Albatross ;* but we are not sure that it
is her after all."

" D'ye notice his maintopmast-staysail, Harry ?"

returned he ; "cut like a trysail, and set on a stay that leads down just clear of his fore-top and into the slings of his fore-yard. How many vessels will ye see with a sail shaped like that ? Yet I noticed that *his* was the other day. And there's the red ribbon round him too ; in fact, it's the *Albatross* all over," concluded he, with the glass once more at his eye.

It was but too evident that Bob was right. I had been hoping that the general resemblance of the brig in sight to the *Albatross* was purely accidental ; but she was now within less than three miles of us ; and, even without the aid of the telescope, certain features, if I may so term them, were recognisable, which identified her beyond all question as the pirate brig.

"What shall we do about answering his signal, Bob ?" said I.

"Let it fly as it is, *un*answered," he replied composedly. "Look where we're dropping him to ; in another quarter of an hour we shall have him fairly on our lee-beam, and that too out of gunshot, unless, as is most likely the case, he's got a long gun ; but if he *has*, we're a small mark to fire at, and we'll soon slip out of range even of that."

It was by this time perfectly manifest that whatever he might be able to do in a breeze, he had no chance with us in a light air like the present; and I entertained strong hopes of being able to slip past him unscathed, when I felt sanguine of our ability to get fairly away from him in a chase dead to windward.

But he evidently had no notion of letting us have our own way in this matter, without a pretty vigorous protest on his part; for as we were still watching him, we saw the brig slowly luff into the wind; his fore-sheet was raised for a moment, a flash of flame and a puff of white smoke darted suddenly from his forecastle, and then we saw the jets spouting up where the shot struck the water, as it came ricocheting towards us. He had aimed apparently so as to throw the shot across our fore-foot; but it fell short by about fifty feet.

"Do that again, you lubber!" exclaimed Bob, contemptuously apostrophising the brig. "Three more such fool's tricks as that, and we'll say

good-bye t'ye without ever having been within
range. See how long it takes him to pay off
ag'in, Harry ; very near lost his way altogether,
when he'd a had to box her off with his head-
yards ; and by the time he'd done that we should
be well clear of him. Well, I *did* think the
man had more sense than to do the like of
that."

Friend Johnson evidently saw his mistake as
clearly as we did, for he fired no more until we
had crept up fairly ahead of him. Just as we
were crossing his bows, however, and had got
his masts in one—by which time he had drawn
considerably nearer us—the brig *fell off* a little,
not to repeat her former error, and again came
the flash, the smoke, and the ringing report.

" Here it comes straight for us this time, and
no mistake," exclaimed Bob, as the water-jets
again marked the course of the shot. " Scald-
ings ! out of the road all of us that's got thin
skulls," continued he, as the shot came skipping
across the water in such long bounds as showed
we were within range. " Well missed !" added

he, as the shot struck the water close to us, and bounded fairly over the boat, passing close beneath the main-boom and the foot of the mainsail, without injuring so much as a rope-yarn.

"That's his long gun, Bob," said I; "his broadside guns would never reach so far as this, and though we're just now in rather warm quarters, we shall be out of range again very soon; and then, I think, we need give ourselves no further trouble concerning him. Any way, you've got something very like the fulfilment of the wish you expressed the other day."

"Ay, ay, that's true, Hal, I have," answered he, with a quiet laugh; "and I *do* own it's a great satisfaction to me that we're carcumventin' the chap this 'a way. I'll warrant he's walking the quarter-deck at this minute fit to bite his fingers off wi' vexation at our slipping past him in this style."

Here another shot from the brig came bounding after us; but we offered him a much smaller mark than before, inasmuch as he was now nearly dead astern of us, and we consequently presented an *end* instead of a broadside view to him.

The shot shaved us pretty close to windward nevertheless, striking the water for the last time just short of our taffrail, and scurrying along and ploughing up the surface close enough to give us a pretty copious shower-bath of spray ere it finally sank just ahead of us.

The next shot, which quickly followed, passed almost as close to leeward ; and the third came straight enough, but fell just short of us.

After this he fired no more.

" Very cleverly managed, I call that, Harry," said Bob, as soon as we found ourselves once more out of range. " We can now take things quietly ; and as it's your watch below, I'd recommend you to turn in and get a bit of a snooze. It's your eight hours out to-night, my lad, and if the breeze should happen to freshen about sundown, and that chap comes after us—and, by the piper, he means that same, for I'm blest if he isn't in stays—you'll need to keep both eyes open all your watch."

This was good advice, and I at once proceeded to adopt it, cautioning Bob to be sure to call me without delay in the event of any further complication arising.

I had not been below above two minutes when I heard his voice shouting to me to come on deck again. Wondering what was now in the wind, I sprang up the short companion-ladder, and my eye at once falling upon the brig (which was now dead astern of us, heading in the same direction as ourselves, though not lying so close to the wind), I saw in a moment that our troubles were not yet by any means over.

The wind had by this time fallen so light that we were not making above three knots' way through the water, whilst the pirate appeared barely to have steerage-way—in fact, his canvas was flapping to the mast with every sluggish roll which the vessel took over the long, scarcely perceptible swell.

Friend Johnson was evidently greatly nettled at our having slipped so handsomely through his fingers as we had, and seemed determined to have a word or two with us yet, whether we would or no; for he had lowered one of his boats, and she was just leaving the vessel in chase.

I took the glass, and counted six men at the oars, besides one or two (I could not be sure which) in the stern-sheets.

This was serious indeed ; for a light boat, propelled by six good oarsmen, would go about two feet to our one at our then rate of sailing, and must necessarily soon overhaul us.

Our case appeared pretty nearly desperate ; but a seaman never gives up " whilst there is a shot in the locker," or a fresh expedient to be tried. So I directed Bob to keep the cutter away about three points, and then lash the tiller, and lend me a hand to get our balloon canvas set.

The topsail was shifted in next to no time, and then we got the spinnaker to the bowsprit-end, leading the sheet aft to the main-boom ; after which we took in our jib and stopped it along the bowsprit, ready for setting again at a moment's notice, and hauled down our staysail.

This additional spread of canvas, coupled with the fact that we were running far enough off the wind to permit of its drawing well, made a perceptible difference in our speed—quite a knot, I considered, and Bob agreed with me.

" Now, what's the next thing to be done, Harry ?" inquired he, as soon as we had completed our task of shifting the sails. " This is all very well as far as it goes, but yon boat is overhauling us at every stroke of the oars, and we've only *postponed* the pleasure of an introduction to the chaps, unless the breeze happens to freshen up a trifle, of which I sees no signs just at present."

" I've made up my mind," I replied. " We *must not* be taken, Bob. I feel convinced that our lives would not be worth an hour's purchase if we fell into the hands of that villain ; but, even supposing he *were* to stop short of murder, his malignity would doubtless prompt him to destroy the little *Lily ;* and by such an act all our past efforts would be nullified, and our future success rendered extremely doubtful. We must *fight* Robert, my man, now that we can no longer run ; so let's get our gun up and rigged without further delay. By the time that we have it ready, they will be within range ; and I think we may persuade them to turn back yet."

" So be it," replied Bob gleefully. " I'd always

rather fight than run away, Harry, lad—at least, when it's anything like a fair match ; so let's rouse up the pop-gun and have a shy at 'em."

This gun was, as I think I have mentioned before, a four-pound rifled piece, which was specially made to my order by an eminent firm. It was a most beautiful little weapon, exquisitely finished ; was a breech-loader, and threw a solid shot about a mile, and a shell nearly half as far again. It was mounted on a swivel or pivot, which we had the means of firmly fixing to the deck.

We got it out and upon deck, and soon had it mounted and ready for service. Bob took the tiller, desiring me to work the gun, as I was not only a more practised artillerist than he, but knew also how to handle a breech-loader, and I had the knack somehow of shooting straight.

I had it loaded, and was in the act of levelling it, when Bob said, " Suppose we was to let them chaps get a bit nearer, Hal, afore we opens fire. I've a notion that if we gets 'em well away from the brig, and well within range of our little barker there, we might give 'em such a peppering afore they could get clear of us ag'in as would sicken 'em of having any more to do with us. Perhaps it mightn't be quite onpossible to destr'y the boat altogether, and then there's seven or eight good hands wiped off the chap's books. This here ain't like a ordinary enemy, you see, lad—he's a sort of general enemy to all mankind ; and the more harm we can do to *him*, the more good we'll be doing the rest of the world."

It sounded rather like cold-blooded barbarity, this proposal of Bob's to attempt the *destruction* instead of the *repulse* of the boat in pursuit of us, but every word he said in support of his proposition was strictly true ; and indeed some such idea had been present in my own mind, so I withheld my fire for a time.

At length, however, they were within half a mile of us, and I thought we might now fairly commence operations. I carefully levelled the piece accordingly, and desiring Bob to sit well out of the line of fire and steer as steadily as possible, I watched the heave of the cutter, and pulled the trigger-line.

The shot sped straight for the boat, but, striking the water just before it reached her, bounded clear over her and into the sea beyond. There was a shout from the people in the boat, and we could see that they stretched to their oars with doubled exertion.

"Straight as it could go, Harry, lad, but *rather* too much elevation; try 'em again, boy, and look smart about it too, for they're giving way as if the devil was behind 'em."

"Which he probably *is*, if they did but know it, Bob," returned I. "Keep cool, old man; there's no hurry; you attend to the steering of the craft, I'll undertake to cool their courage for them before they're very much older."

"Ay, ay," retorted Bob, "keep cool it is; but it's getting to be rather ticklish work, lad, ain't it?"

I was too busy with the gun to reply just then, and in another moment I fired once more. This time we saw the splinters fly from the bows of the boat, and one of the oarsmen sprang from his seat and fell back into the arms of the man behind him.

There was a moment of confusion with them, and then we saw one of the men in the stern-sheets (there *were* two of them) step along the thwarts and take the injured man's place. This looked like a fixed determination to come alongside at any price, so I this time inserted a shell instead of a solid shot, which I had before been firing.

Once more, after a very careful aim, the little piece rang out, and again the shot reached its mark; this time with terrible effect, for the shell exploded as it passed through the boat's thin planking, and the fragments, continuing their flight forward, told so severely among the crew that it appeared as if they were *all* more or less hurt. We saw four fall from the thwarts, at all events, and all hands ceased pulling, whilst three of the oars slipped unnoticed overboard.

I unrove the spinnaker-sheet from the main-boom before the astonished Bob knew what I was about, let go the halliards, and let the sail down by the run; and then jumped to the jib halliards and hoisted the sail like lightning.

"Now," shouted I, "luff you may, Bob, and

let's heave the craft to, and finish the job for them."

As I said this, Bob put his helm down, whilst I hauled the jib sheet to windward, and then I sprang aft again to the gun.

By this time they had taken to their oars again, but there were only two of them pulling : a sure indication of the extent to which our last shot had told.   They were turning the boat round to pull back to the ship, and seeing this I felt some compunction about firing on them again, and said so.

" Don't be such a soft-hearted donkey, Harry, lad," retorted Bob.   " Settle the whole lot if you can, boy ; it'll only be so many skulking cut-throats the less in the world.   *My* idee is that every one of them chaps as we can finish off is one honest man's life saved ; so give 'em another of them shells, my boy.   They *do* seem wonderful persuaders, small as they be."

I accordingly loaded again, and fired ; but, probably from excitement, fired too high, and the missile flew harmlessly over the boat.

The next time I was more careful, aiming with

the utmost deliberation. At length I pulled the trigger-line, and immediately leapt to my feet to watch for the result.

The shell struck the boat's stern fairly amidships, and close to the water-line; there was an explosion, but both the oarsmen appeared to be unhurt. Almost immediately, however, one of them sprang aft and crouched down, doing something that we could not make out.

I took the glass, and then saw that a large gap had been made by the explosion of the shell, through which the water was doubtless pouring rapidly.

There was a movement among the wounded men; and one man jumped upon a thwart and waved his hat to the brig, evidently as a signal of distress. Her captain had of course been watching us all this time, and seemed to have conjectured that his people were getting the worst of it, for we now saw that he had a second boat in the water; and on taking a look at the brig through the glass, we observed that he had a tackle on his main yard-arm, with which he was hoisting out a gun to put into the boat.

" It is time we were off once more, Bob," I remarked, as soon as I saw this ; " so another shot at our friends here, and then we'll fill away."

The boat was very much disabled, and appeared to be sinking gradually, notwithstanding their efforts to keep her afloat, for they were now baling rapidly ; but I thought it best to make sure of her, so once more loaded and fired.

The shell passed through her stern this time also, and exploded ; there was a shrill scream from more than one agonised throat, and the baling and pulling ceased altogether ; every man in her was wounded, if not killed outright.

Satisfied with our work of destruction, and not particularly caring to expose ourselves to the fire of the gun in the other boat, which was no doubt much heavier than our own toy of a weapon, we filled away ; and I once more swayed up the spinnaker forward, desiring Bob to keep just sufficiently away to permit of our balloon canvas fully drawing, but no more.

As soon as I had got the spinnaker set, I took the glass and had a good look at the boat we had beaten off. She was nearly full of water, her gunwale being but an inch or two above the surface.

I saw three or four figures rouse themselves on board her, and recommence baling feebly; but their efforts were useless; she sank lower and lower, and at length rolled heavily bottom upwards, throwing her wounded crew into the water.

Almost immediately there was a furious splashing, and by the aid of the glass I distinctly saw the dorsal fins of several sharks darting here and there among them, whilst over the glassy surface of the water a shriek or two came faintly towards us.

In less than a minute all was over with the miserable wretches; the voracious sharks made short work of it with them, tearing living and dead alike to pieces in their eagerness to obtain a share of the prey.

At the moment that this tragic scene was enacting, the second boat was about half-way between the brig and those to whose assistance she was hastening; and her crew had a nearer and more distinct view of the horrible details of the catastrophe than we had.

They paused for a moment on their oars as though paralysed with horror; and then with a vengeful shout gave way more energetically than before.

But I felt little apprehension on their account; the dying breeze had revived somewhat, and the *Lily* was now stealing along, though with scarcely a ripple at her sharp bows, about five knots; and the water looked rather darker to windward, as though the wind was inclined to come still stronger.

The pirates tugged at their oars with might and main, passing within oar's length of the wreck of the first boat, when they again raised a furious yell, straining away at their stout ash blades until they made them bend like willow wands.

They gained on us considerably within the first ten minutes or quarter of an hour; and I saw some of the crew preparing to fire the gun which was mounted in the boat's bows. Judging that more powder would have to be burned after all,

I once more loaded our little piece, charging with shell as before; and whilst I was doing this our pursuers opened fire upon us.

They miscalculated their distance, however, or the powers of their gun; for the shot fell considerably short of us, much to Bob's delight, to which he gave expression by the utterance of a few remarks of such biting sarcasm and raillery that they would infallibly have still further incensed the individuals to whom they were addressed could they but have heard them.

I too was *very* glad to see the shot fall short, for it placed us on somewhat more equal terms than I had dared to hope. The boat was a large one, probably their launch, and pulled ten oars; and there were three men in the bows working the gun, and the coxswain aft steering, making altogether fourteen hands—very heavy odds.

But then, on the other hand, the boat was heavy, and her crew, after their already long pull, could not maintain the violent exertions they were now putting forth very much longer; and a very trifling abatement in that direction would enable us to slip away from them after all; and, moreover, as they were now within range of our gun (which, being rifled, threw a shot much farther than their smooth-bore), there was a possibility of our being able so far to disable them as to compel them to give up the chase.

I accordingly levelled the breech-loader, and then waited for a favourable opportunity to fire. At length it came. The shell entered the starboard bow of the pursuing boat, about midway between her gunwale and her water-line; and immediately, to our great surprise, there was a violent explosion on board her.

A vivid flash of flame darted upward and outward; the sides of the boat appeared to be violently wrenched apart at their junction with the stem; the gun and its carriage rose heavily in the air about ten feet, and fell with a tremendous splash into the sea; and oars and men were flung wildly about, many of them being blown fairly overboard, whilst a dense cloud of smoke arose, and for a moment hid everything from our view.

When it cleared away, there floated the wreck of the boat, just awash ; and there too, among the struggling crew in the water, darted to and fro the fins of the terrible sharks, very probably the same monsters who had so recently feasted on their shipmates. Our shell had taken most fearful effect, igniting their ammunition, and thus blowing their boat to pieces at our first discharge.

CHAPTER XI.

THE CHASE DIVERTED.

THERE was an awful suddenness about the destruction of this second boat and her crew which almost appalled us, and it was with considerably sobered feelings that, after a dead silence of a few minutes, we proceeded to discuss the character of our next movements.

Our proper course was about north-west, that being the bearing of the point, the latitude and longitude of which had been given us as that of the treasure island.

Our charts showed no island exactly at that spot, but there were many at very short distances from it; indeed it was situated almost in the very heart of that extensive group of islets known as the Low Archipelago ; and when talking the matter over before, we had decided that it was quite possible we should be obliged to take a somewhat extended cruise among these islands, and to examine several of them before coming upon the one of which we were in search.

Under these circumstances we came to the conclusion that it would be unadvisable to give the pirates any indication of our true destination by steering on our proper course as long as they were in sight, for the destruction of their two boats, with the loss of their crews, would undoubtedly kindle such a desire for vengeance in the breasts of the survivors as, in all likelihood, to prompt them to go a good bit out of their way, if necessary, to get it.

So, after a long debate and a careful examination of the chart, which I brought on deck for the purpose, we decided to bear away on a course as though bound to New Zealand.

This took us about a point farther off the wind than we had been steering for the last few hours; but we did not trouble much about that, as we hoped to give the brig the slip some time during the ensuing night.

Accordingly we bore away upon the course decided on; the sails were trimmed with the utmost nicety, and then, it being about the time for our evening meal, I took the tiller, while Bob went below to look after the kettle.

The brig was by this time about six or seven miles astern of us, and was steering directly after us, with apparently every stitch of canvas set that would draw. I lashed the tiller for a moment, and jumped down below for my sextant, with which I returned to the deck, and carefully set him by it, with the view of ascertaining just before dark whether he had gained anything on us, or we on him, in the interim.

Tea being ready, Bob served it on deck; and whilst we leisurely discussed the meal, we talked over our chances of dodging our pursuer during the night.

Unfortunately, these now appeared to be rather

slender ; for there was not a cloud to be seen, and the moon, well advanced in her second quarter, was already visible in the deep sapphire of the eastern sky ere the west had well begun to glow with the rich warm hues of sunset. And to add to our difficulty in this respect, the wind again fell lighter, and ere long died completely away.

The sun went down in calm and cloudless splendour ; the golden glories of the west deepened into rich crimson, then faded into purple, and from purple into warm grey ; the brief twilight quickly deepened into night, and the moon, " sweet regent of the sky," shed her soft silvery beams abroad over the tranquil ocean ; while the larger stars added their mellow radiance to beautify the scene.

There was not the faintest breath of wind to ruffle the mirror-like surface of the long glassy swells as they undulated sluggishly beneath us ; and the flap of our canvas, the pattering of the reef-points, the creaking of the main-boom, and the occasional "*cheep, cheep*" of the rudder upon its pintles, served but to mark and emphasise the deep calm of sleeping Nature.

It was a glorious night—a night of such exquisite loveliness as is perhaps never witnessed except when far away from land; but, situated as we were, greatly as we admired its beauty, we would rather have witnessed a sky traversed by fast-flying clouds, and would gladly have exchanged the tender silence which brooded around us for the singing of the wind through our rigging and the hissing sound of the rapidly following surges.

We walked fore and aft on our short deck, one on each side, smoking our pipes and whistling for a breeze, and pausing occasionally to listen for the roll of oars in their rowlocks, or their plash in the water; for we did not know what new trick our neighbour astern might feel disposed to play us, though we both thought it improbable he would send another boat away—at all events, whilst we maintained our present distance from him.

He was distinctly visible in the bright moonlight, and of course we kept a watchful eye upon him; but we could detect no signs aboard of him to give us any uneasiness.

At length, just about eight bells, as Bob was

preparing to go below, I noticed that the shimmer of the moonbeams, which had hitherto played in but a few wavering streaks over the surface of the water close to us, was now revealing itself on the horizon, spreading gradually abroad on each side of the point at which it had first appeared, and slowly advancing over the surface of the ocean towards us.

"Here comes the breeze, Bob!" I exclaimed. "Stay on deck a few minutes longer until we can see what is to be the order of the night. See, there it comes, away out from the eastward; and the brig is already squaring away his yards, as though he felt the first faint puffs. Ay," continued I, as I took a look at him through the glass, "there go his stunsail-booms, and there go his stunsails to boot. Now the rascal will run down to us with the first of the breeze, and perhaps have us under his guns before we can catch a breath of it. Cast loose this spinnaker-boom, old man, and let's get it rigged out and the sail set in readiness for the breeze when it comes. If we can only get it before he comes within range of us, I believe we can walk away from him even in a run to leeward, provided we don't have the breeze *too* strong."

We worked with a will, the reader may be sure, and soon had the huge sail set on the starboard side, whilst the main-boom was guyed out to port.

We then went all round the deck, taking a pull at the halliards where necessary ; and then, though a heavy dew was falling, we got up a small hand-pump and some hose we had provided ourselves with, and gave the sails a thorough wetting.

The brig ran down to within about a couple of miles of us before the first faint cat's-paws came stealing over the water towards us ; then the bal-loon-topsail filled, collapsed, and filled again, the spinnaker ceased its rustle, and there was a gentle surge as the light strain first came upon the spars and rigging ; the tiller began to vibrate beneath my hand, a long ripple spread itself out from each bow, and the *Water Lily* began once more to slip gaily away.

I got Bob to give a look to our preventers, in case it should become a matter of sheer *carrying on*, and then sent him below, as it had been a day of excitement for him, and, consequently, of fatigue.

The breeze gradually freshened, the water hissed and sparkled away from our sharp bows, and the swirling eddies in our wake told a cheering tale as to the speed with which we were flying over the surface of the now crisply-ruffled ocean ; and before my watch was out, I had the satisfaction of seeing that we were certainly drawing away from our persevering enemy, the broad, flat model of the *Lily* being as favourable to her sailing powers before the wind as her deep keel was when close-hauled.

I called Bob at midnight, and strictly cautioned him to give me timely notice if the breeze freshened sufficiently to necessitate a reduction of canvas, or if anything occurred rendering my presence on deck desirable ; and then I dived below, flung off my clothes, and tumbled into my hammock, and "in the twinkling of a purser's lantern" was fast asleep.

When I went on deck again at four o'clock I found that the breeze had freshened very considerably during my watch below, and under other circumstances I should most certainly have taken in the spinnaker and shifted topsails; but though we had dropped the brig considerably, he still hung most pertinaciously in our wake, so there was nothing for it but still to carry on.

The craft must have been a splendid sailer, for, though by this time we were going close upon sixteen knots, we had not increased our distance from her much more than four miles during the time I had been below.

Nothing worthy of note occurred during my watch. The wind appeared to have reached the limits of its strength, and now blew steadily, with sufficient force to try our spars and gear to their utmost, but not quite strong enough to carry anything away, and we continued to increase our distance from the brig.

At seven bells I called Bob, who set about the preparations for breakfast, and great were our mutual congratulations over that meal at the now thoroughly-established fact that, fast as the *Albatross* undoubtedly was, she was no match for the little *Water Lily* in ordinary weather.

As soon as breakfast was over and the things

cleared away, I got an observation for the longitude, and then went below to have a nap, desiring Bob to call me at seven bells, that I might take a meridian altitude.

He did so, and as soon as I came on deck with my sextant, he said, " Look there, Harry, what d'ye think of that ? I wouldn't call ye when I first made 'em out, as it only wanted half an hour to seven bells, and I knowed you'd feel a bit tired after yesterday. But *ain't* it a wonderful sight ?"

As he spoke he pointed away to a little on our starboard bow, and stooping down in order to see under the foot of the spinnaker, I there beheld what was indeed to me a wonderful sight. Away nearly as far as we could see, upon the verge of the horizon, appeared a vast herd or " school " of whales, spouting in all directions and indulging in the most extraordinary gambols, each apparently striving to outvie the others in the feat of leaping entirely out of the water.

I am afraid to make anything like a positive statement as to the heights achieved by some of the monsters, but it really appeared to me that a

few of them rose nearly, if not quite, five and
twenty feet into the air, descending again with a
splash which reminded me of some of the torpedo
experiments I had witnessed when staying for a
few days at Portsmouth.

I was careful to get my observation, which I
rapidly worked out, and entered in the log; after
which I relieved Bob at the tiller, whilst he went
below to see to the dinner.

As he descended the short companion-ladder
he turned round and observed with a comical
look, "I say, Harry, I hope there ain't no stray
sarpents knocking about in this here neighbour-
hood; 'twould be uncommon awk'ard for us to
have one of they chaps waiting for us ahead and
that infarnal brig still in sight astarn."

Just as dinner made its appearance I descried a
sail about two points on our starboard bow. It
was a vessel under single-reefed topsails, heading
to the southward, and consequently standing
across our bows.

She was too far off for us to make out anything
but the heads of her sails from the deck, but as
soon as I saw her I resigned the tiller to Bob and

went up as far as the crosstrees to have a better look at her.

From thence I made her out to be a barque apparently close hauled on the port tack; but of what nationality she might be we were yet too far distant from her to decide, though I thought from the cut of her sails that she was English.

I was still standing upon the crosstrees, shouting my observations to Bob, when I noticed a commotion amongst the herd of whales, which we were by this time fast nearing, and bringing my glass to bear, I at length made out three boats pulling towards them.

The whales were evidently rather doubtful as to the intentions of these boats, though we were not. We saw at once that the stranger was a whaler, and that these were her boats despatched in chase.

The whales came swimming leisurely to windward with the boats in hot pursuit. What to do was now the question with us. We ought most certainly to advise the whalers of the character of the brig, but it would never do to shorten sail and deviate anything considerable from our course with this object.

We should very probably be taken before we could accomplish our purpose, and in that event we should sacrifice ourselves without doing the others any good. However, as a preliminary, we displayed our ensign, and as the boats were coming almost directly towards us, I sheered sufficiently out of our course to pass within hail of the leader.

We were now running through the very thickest of the herd, and it was rather nervous work, for with a single lash of its mighty tail any one of the monsters might have destroyed us; and with such a cloud of canvas as we were carrying the deviations from our course which we dared to make were very trifling.

Had we luffed, for example, high enough for our spinnaker to jibe, the craft would probably have "turned the turtle" with us; or, if we had proved fortunate enough to escape this, we should most certainly have made a clean sweep of the spars.

We were almost within hail of the leading

boat when she fastened to an enormous whale. The creature dived instantly, taking out line at a tremendous rate, but still continuing on its original course.

This brought the boat close past us on our starboard side, the crew sitting with their oars apeak, and the water foaming a good foot above the level of the boat's bows as she was towed furiously along.

I took the trumpet in my hand, and as she dashed past, I hailed, "The brig astern is a pirate ; cut adrift and rejoin your ship as soon as possible."

The boat-steerer waved his hand, but they made no attempt to free themselves from the whale, and I feared they had not clearly understood me ; though I saw the men turning to each other as though comparing notes on the communication I had made, and the boat-steerer shaded his eyes with his hand as he took a hasty look at the rapidly approaching brig.

The two other boats, meanwhile, were pulling away to the southward in pursuit of a couple of gigantic whales which had 'separated from the rest of the herd, and which, from the pace at which they were travelling, seemed likely to lead their pursuers a pretty dance. It was quite out of our power to convey any warning to those, and I was most reluctantly compelled to stand on upon our original course, or dead to leeward.

Presently the whale which was struck turned sharp round, and came tearing back over the ground he had just traversed. I felt more than half inclined to take as broad a sheer as I dared out of his way; I did not at all like the look of him as he came foaming down towards us.

But the desire to repeat my warning was stronger even than my fear of the whale; and, watching him narrowly as he came up, I directed Bob how to steer, and the instant he was past us, Bob eased down the helm, and we sheered towards the boat he had in tow.

I stood by with the trumpet as before, but it was unnecessary, for as they came alongside, the boat-steerer sheered our way, whilst the crew rapidly paid out line, by which means the whale-boat's speed was so reduced that we had time to communicate before she passed ahead.

"Cutter ahoy!" hailed the boat-steerer as we rushed along within twenty feet of each other; "what was that you said just now?"

"The brig astern of us is a pirate," I replied; "she fired upon us yesterday at midday, and has been in chase ever since. I would advise you to rejoin your ship before she comes up if possible. Your skipper will need all his hands on board if she ranges alongside."

"The devil!" ejaculated he in reply. "You don't seem hit anywhere," glancing aloft at our taper spars and snowy canvas, which showed no wounds or shot-holes to vouch for the truth of my statement.

"No," answered I; "he only had time to fire five shots at us before we slipped past him to windward, and we escaped untouched."

"Hang it!" he exclaimed, in a tone of vexation; "I don't like to lose this fine fish that we're fast to; but we shall have to let him go, no doubt of that; but how the devil am I to recall the other boats?"

" I will fire our gun to attract their attention,"
I replied, "and you can make any signal you think
most likely to effect your object."

" Thank 'ee," returned he ; " I shall be obliged
if you will."

And then he signalled to the men who had
charge of the line, and they gradually reduced
the speed at which it ran out, and finally held
all fast with an extra turn round the bollard, and
away the boat dashed once more.

I charged the gun (which still remained
mounted on deck) with a blank cartridge, and
duly greasing the muzzle to increase the report,
fired. The crew of the whale-boat tossed their
oars on end, and kept them so for a few minutes,
or until it was seen that the other boats had
abandoned the chase, and were pulling back
toward them.

The crew of the boat which was fast to the
whale were knowing enough not to cut themselves
adrift so long as their prize towed them in the
direction they wished to go ; and, as he seemed
to have started for a regular long run to leeward,

they appeared to stand a very fair chance of being towed almost alongside their ship.

She had been making short stretches to windward ever since we first sighted her, and we were by this time within a couple of miles of her. From her motions we judged that the people left on board to work her had heard the report of our gun, and had witnessed the recall of the other two boats, and perhaps suspected that something was wrong somewhere, for she was now plainly manœuvring to close with all three of the boats as quickly as possible.

The whale, meanwhile, had been running in such a direction as to cross the barque's bows about a quarter of a mile distant, and he actually ran far enough to enable the crew of the boat which had fastened to him to cut themselves adrift when fairly in their ship's course; so that, in a very few minutes after the stroke of the keen tomahawk had severed their towline, they were alongside, and the boat was run up to the davits.

So smart were the crew of the whaler in picking up their boat, that they must have swung their mainyard the moment the frail craft was hooked on, without waiting until she was actually hoisted up.

The barque had scarcely begun to gather way before the hands were in her rigging, and next moment they were laying out on both topsail-yards and turning out the reefs ; although the breeze was so strong that, half-loaded as she was, she was careening almost gunwale to.

We passed close under her stern ; and her skipper, as we drew near, walked aft to the taffrail and hailed us.

" Thank you, sir, for your information ; please report us and this circumstance ; God knows whether we shall escape the rascals or no."

I waved my hand, to signify that I understood and would comply with his request ; noting, as I did so, the name and the port of registry of the vessel, which were painted on her stern in white letters : " The *Kingfisher*, of Hull."

Scarcely were we past her, when we saw a small red flag go fluttering up to her main-topgallant-masthead; a signal, as we supposed, to hurry the other boats back. The poor fellows were awkwardly situated.

Had they been hull-down to the northward or the southward, the pirates might possibly, in the eagerness of their desire for vengeance upon us, have allowed her to pass on unmolested; but now that the barque lay almost directly within their path, we dared not hope for any such display of forbearance.

There were many stores on board a well-found whaler which would be most useful to men situated like the desperadoes on board the brig; and they would scarcely forego the opportunity of making the acquisition for the sake of continuing to chase a craft which was indubitably walking away from them fast, and which must run them out of sight altogether in a few hours more, unless some accident occurred to place her within their power.

We watched the proceedings of the two vessels

with the most absorbing interest, as may well be supposed. The *Lily* was very quickly far enough to leeward of the barque to enable us to see the two boats clear of his bow; and we noticed that their crews were pulling with might and main.

But in about ten minutes' time they were once more shut in by the intervention of their vessel's hull between us and them; and before they could open out astern of her, the barque went in stays, having apparently stood on far enough to fetch her boats on the next tack.

The brig had in the interim run down to within about four miles of the whaler, and was still flying along, dead before the wind, with everything set, up to topgallant stunsails on both sides; and no sign had so far revealed itself on board her by which we could judge of the intention of her crew.

By the time that she had run another mile, we saw the whaler's main-yard once more thrown aback; an indication that she was about to pick up her other two boats; and there now appeared to be a strong probability that she would have time to hoist them in and be off again, before the pirate could approach her within gun-shot.

The situation became eminently exciting ; and so anxious was I that the whaler should have every chance of making her escape, that I directed Bob to let go our spinnaker out-haul, and allow the traveller to run in along the boom, in the hope that, by leading the pirates to believe it had become necessary for us to shorten sail, they might be tempted, after all, to keep on in chase of us, instead of interfering with the barque.

It would have afforded us almost unmitigated satisfaction to have seen them continue the chase, for we now felt perfectly satisfied that in moderate weather we had the heels of the *Albatross*, both close-hauled and running free, and could we succeed in decoying them far enough to lee-ward to permit of the whaler making good his escape, I was willing to trust to the future for the means of ultimately shaking our vindictive pursuer off.

In further prosecution of this project, as soon as Bob had got the spinnaker in, I lashed the

tiller for a moment and jumped forward to assist
him in getting in our enormous balloon topsail,
which I foresaw would have to be taken off the
craft shortly if we wished to save the topmast, the
wind being rather on the increase and our rigging
already strained to the tension of harp-strings.
This done, we found time to take another look at
the whaler.

His main-yard was just swinging as we turned
our glances in his direction, and then his bows fell
off until he headed about north-west; his men
springing into the rigging and scurrying away
aloft to loose topgallant-sails; one hand meantime
laying out on the jibboom to loose the flying-
jib.

Away went the jolly old craft in magnificent
style, heading about north-west, and evidently
upon her best point of sailing. She crossed our
stern, shutting out the pirate brig for a moment,
and we fully expected that when that craft next
appeared we should see her hauled up in chase;
but nothing of the kind; on she came, still heading
direct for us, and I began to hope that our plan

of luring her on to follow us was about to prove successful.

Two or three minutes, which seemed like ages to us, elapsed; and then, all in a moment, his stunsails (or *studding*-sails, as I ought more correctly to spell the word) collapsed, and fluttered wildly for a few seconds in the breeze, and disappeared; his royal-halliards were let go, and the sails rolled up and furled; and as he hauled up to follow the barque, his foresail lifted and there was a flash, a puff of white smoke, and before the report had time to drive down to us we saw the shot skipping along from wave to wave, as a polite intimation to the barque to heave to.

But the whaling skipper was not the man to give up without a struggle. He had no studding-sails, but he was heading in such a direction that the brig could not use hers while following him, and it seemed that he trusted to his light trim to enable him to get clear.

Gun after gun was now rapidly fired by the pirates, but they were not yet within range, though it was only too evident that they would be before very long, and I greatly feared that the barque's chances of escape were remarkably small.

In about an hour they both disappeared in the north-western board; but, when last seen, the barque was still carrying on, with the pirate banging away at her most perseveringly with his long gun.

"Thank goodness, we're shut of the blackguards at last!" exclaimed Bob, as the sails of the two craft sank below the horizon; "though I'm duberous it's a poor look-out for them whalin' chaps. If the poor beggars gets caught, it's small marcy as they'll have showed 'em, unless there's any on 'em white-livered enough to jine the brig to save their lives. Skipper Johnson won't be partic'lar amiable, I reckon, a'ter the loss of his two boats' crews yesterday—two-and-twenty hands, all told; and I don't suppose as he's the man to mind much *who* he has his revenge upon, so long's he *gets* it. But what's to be our next move, lad, now we're once more all alone by ourselves?"

"I've been thinking about that," I replied. "I do not expect the pirates will trouble their heads

about us any more, now that they have lost sight
of us ; but they *may*, and it will be just as well to
provide against any such contingency. If they re-
sume the chase, they will most probably look for
us somewhere on the course we were steering
when last seen, or else to the northward. There
is nothing to take us to the southward, so that is
the most improbable direction, in my opinion, in
which they are likely to look for us ; and that,
therefore, is the direction in which I propose to
steer. Let us make the craft snug, and stand
away to the southward and eastward, full and by,
and at eight o'clock to-morrow morning we will go
about and make a leg to the northward and eastward for perhaps twenty-four hours. This will
place us well to windward, and in about the last
spot in the world where he would think of looking
for us. What do you think of the plan, Bob ?"

" Fust rate," responded that worthy ; " a reg'lar
traverse, and about the most in-and-out bit of car-
cumvention as the ingenuity o' man could invent.
Let's set about it at once, my lad ; and by the
time as we've cleared up a bit, and made things

comfortable, it'll be time to see about gettin' tea."

We accordingly set about " making things comfortable " forthwith. The balloon-topsail was carefully rolled up and put away, the spinnaker (which we had only allowed to run in close to the mast, and had hastily secured with a stop or two) ditto, and our topmast housed ; the spinnaker-boom was run in, unrigged, and secured, and we then gibed the mainsail over, and stood away, close-hauled, about south-east, the little *Lily* staggering along in regular racing style under whole lower canvas, when by rights, with the amount of wind we had, we ought to have had at least *one* reef down, and the No. 1 jib shifted for No. 2.

However, we were used to carrying on by this time, and had become so thoroughly intimate with the cutter's sail-carrying powers that we knew we might safely give her all the canvas her spars would bear.

By the time that all was done, and our gun (which we did not think it worth while to dismount and stow away again for the present) carefully covered over with its painted canvas coat, the sun was on the verge of the horizon, the weather having a settled appearance, with a promise of the breeze holding good through the night.

END OF VOL. I.

BILLING AND SONS, PRINTERS, GUILDFORD, SURREY.

www.ingramcontent.com/pod-product-compliance
Lightning Source LLC
Chambersburg PA
CBHW021039030726
47496CB00006B/1606